Maguni's Bullock Cart & Other Classic Odia Stories

OTHER BOOKS IN THE SERIES

A Teashop in Kamalapura and Other Classic Kannada Stories
The Second Marriage of Kunju Namboodiri and Other Classic Malayalam Stories

Maguni's Bullock Cart & Other Classic Odia Stories

Series edited by Mini Krishnan
Translated by Leelawati Mohapatra,
Paul St-Pierre and K.K. Mohapatra

HARPER**PERENNIAL**
An Imprint of HarperCollins *Publishers*

First published in India by Harper Perennial 2025
An imprint of HarperCollins *Publishers*
4th Floor, Tower A, Building No. 10, DLF Cyber City,
DLF Phase II, Gurugram, Haryana – 122002
www.harpercollins.co.in

2 4 6 8 10 9 7 5 3 1

English Translation © Leelawati Mohapatra, K.K. Mohapatra,
Paul St-Pierre 2025
A Note on the Series © Mini Krishnan 2025
Copyright for individual stories vests in their respective writers

Though every effort has been made to trace the copyright holders of the stories published in this volume, it has not been possible to do so in all cases. Any omissions brought to our notice will be rectified in future editions.

P-ISBN: 978-93-6569-157-3
E-ISBN: 978-93-6569-225-9

This is a work of fiction and all characters and incidents described in this book are the product of the authors' imagination. Any resemblance to actual persons, living or dead, is entirely coincidental.

Each individual writer asserts the moral right
to be identified as the author of their work.

All rights reserved. No part of this publication may be reproduced, stored in a retrieval system, or transmitted, in any form or by any means, electronic, mechanical, photocopying, recording or otherwise, without the prior permission of the publishers.

Typeset in 11.5/16.2 Adobe Caslon Pro at
HarperCollins *Publishers* India

Printed and bound at
Thomson Press (India) Ltd.

This book is produced from independently certified FSC® paper
to ensure responsible forest management.

To the early pioneers of modern Indian literature—whose pens may not all have carved timeless tales, yet each stroke contributed to the shaping of a nation's voice. Their courage in expression and commitment to storytelling laid the foundation for the literary landscape we cherish today.

CONTENTS

A Note on the Series   ix

Introduction   xv

1898 Fakir Mohan Senapati: REBATI   1

1899 Reba Ray: THE SANYASI   16

1913 Fakir Mohan Senapati: PATENT MEDICINE   27

1914 Lakshmikanta Mahapatra: THE OLD BANGLE-SELLER   39

1914 Godavarish Mishra: HIS BETTER HALF   47

1915 Bankanidhi Patnaik: LACHHAMANJI   55

1924 Upendra Kishore Das: THE FLAME: A GHOST STORY   70

1925 Suprabha Kar: THE LONG WAIT   85

1935 Biswanath Rath: THE WITCH   93

1936 Bhagabati Charan Panigrahi: THE KILL   100

1936 Gopinath Mohanty: DĀ   105

1937 Kanhu Charan Mohanty: THE GNARLED SAHADA TREE   112

CONTENTS

1938 Nityananda Mahapatra: THE QUEST	120
1938 Harischandra Badal: THE TIGER	132
1939 Godavarish Mohapatra: MAGUNI'S BULLOCK CART	144
1939 Satchidananda Routray: FLOWER OF EVIL	149
1945 Kalindi Charan Panigrahi: VICTORY CELEBRATION	156
1945 Rajkishore Ray: BAULI	169
1945 Rajkishore Pattanaik: A HOUSE TO LET	177
1945 Surendra Mohanty: AUSTRALIA	183
Acknowledgements	189
Notes on Authors	191

A NOTE ON THE SERIES

A POEM ABOUT READING begins 'I opened a book and in I strode / Now nobody can find me' and ends by saying 'I finished my book and out I came … But I have a book inside me.' Anyone who has read a work of fiction (is it ever wholly fiction?) knows what it is to return repeatedly to the memory of this or that character or event. Sometimes everything is forgotten except the impression and emotion those pages conjured up. This is particularly true of short stories: literary lightning that tears through you and exits leaving a wordy high.

I collect translated stories the way other people collect watches or potted plants, recipes or paintings, or something that gives them the pleasure of possession; my collection of stories belong to their writers and translators. They possess me. That's just how literature is. Along the way, I have had a whole lot of unoriginal thoughts: Is our portmanteau of words enough to convey the complexity of our lives? Why do some languages appear to have more words than others? How might we convey what cannot be said? Coincidentally,

A NOTE ON THE SERIES

all these questions about language and life apply to the art and effort of translation—some might say trans-adaptation—as well.

The idea for this series came from a collection of Malayalam stories I received from Dr M.M. Basheer, who edited and published *Aadhya Kaalathe Stree Katha* in 2010—stories by early women writers. Why only women, I thought to myself, but there were too many other things to do and deadlines to meet and the moment faded. But the seed was sown. For a while, I rattled along with the idea of a most neglected genre—the long story, which fell between the short story and the novella—until David Davidar published a collection I put together for Aleph Book Company: *Tell Me a Long Long Story* (2017). Five years before that, through Oxford University Press (India), I edited a series of novellas. After I retired, I tried to secure the interest of publishers in volumes of long stories from different Indian languages. Again—closed doors. Very slowly, and around the same time, it became clear that all the big prizes for translated fiction were reserved for novels by living writers. Naturally, publishers shifted focus to the map of that heaven. What, I thought to myself, will happen to those writers who were no longer with us but were the reason we are where we are in terms of tastes, styles, experiments and themes? The sun setting on our literary past, where pre-modern met modern, began to bother me. So, I came up with what I thought was my next big idea—anthologies of EISET: Early Indian Stories in English Translation. Fortunately, my editor, Rahul Soni, saw some potential in this apparently forgotten zone.

The evolution of fiction in Indian languages is linked with the development of prose—in some languages, a relatively recent medium for literary expression. To be sure, storytelling itself evolved from the earliest human societies and is the oldest form of enchantment through entertainment closely linked with song and India's long culture of orality. India had sophisticated poetics and complex orature at a time when modern European languages were just emerging. Tamil, for instance, was a fully developed language thousands of years ago, well before Sanskrit became the power-and-prestige lingua franca. But printed fictional works came to be evaluated largely in terms of their closeness to Western models, and at least eighty years of Indian short fiction from the last quarter of the nineteenth to well into the sixth decade of the twentieth century were strongly influenced by Western norms riveted in place by British models or translations of European works into English. As schools, colleges and popular reading materials proliferated, maintaining the complex balance between the intimate and the universal fell into the hands of the writers and promoters of fiction, projecting as they did an illusion of life and truth, which is the function of Literature. For a very long time in social and academic contexts that reverenced the classics as the only things worth studying, fiction was seen as second-class literature. With this stands the raging question of plural heritage, both local and imported. Was there a conflict? Or a smooth hybridization swallowed whole by a readership from which the writer himself or—on rare occasions—herself originated?

In an interview, Dorothy Figueira said that though early translations were inspired by pragmatic colonial needs to understand Indians better in order to rule and control, it was not entirely unidirectional; Indians responded to commentary from the West. It was a dialogue from the beginning. This was possible probably because the translingual sensibility lies deep in Indians educated in any language, though that immediately reminds me and everybody else that even illiterate populations in our country are effortlessly bilingual. E.V. Ramakrishnan does not agree. In paper after paper, he discusses the massive shifts in the cultural domain when English began to displace Sanskrit as the Indian subcontinent moved towards colonial modernity. He calls this time of cultural and linguistic violence a time of rupture.

It is routinely said and printed that there are more speakers and readers of English in India than there are in the Anglophone world, and the pressure this single language applies today upon our language empire is incalculable. There can be no argument about the fact that the biggest intervention in the social energy of our languages was the arrival of English. At some cost to our languages, while simultaneously enriching us with outside influences, it has nudged us into a sense of needing to keep up with world literature—a trend that has led to a sudden visibility for translations of Indian literary works.

Languages are like opposing reigning powers, and translators are the ambassadors who flit between two kingdoms. The encoding they pack at one end and unpack at the other for another language readership naturally calls for great skills. Translation is a deep reading of a text. Every story or poem has a voice. Inward, human. It asks you to believe the feeling locked into the printed word and it reaches you through your reader-ear. We read as listeners because the origin of stories is orality. Imagine the translator's workshop, created in a phantom space between two languages, in some sense, a linguistic outer space where there do not appear to be any recognizable norms. Monolingual peoples have tried hard to arrive at rules, many of which suit them but most of which break

A NOTE ON THE SERIES

down when translators function in a multilingual context such as ours in India.

Let me say something else here. The multiple flavours and successes of a translation depend a lot on the personality of the translator—how ethical, how vain, how patient, how adventurous they are—to say nothing of that invisible meddler called the editor or facilitator. To plunge within, in order to extrapolate outwardly what another said, calls for utter honesty. No grandstanding or vanity must be allowed to intervene and contaminate the rendering. Is the translator competing with the original or seeking to supplant it? I can never decide, but I do think successful translations run just a little ahead of their originals as if clearing the way for the author, becoming in fact a third entity that is neither the source nor the target language. Gustave Flaubert said that a translation should free itself from the translator; is that—could it be—true? At a time when identities are not only plural but fluid, and we are continuously told what to think and how to think, our translated literature should be seen for what it is and can be: not just a part of history, but a bank, a treasure house of our own pasts because memory is the cement of our identity. The translations in this series offer a rich mix of the music and sounds of some of our languages.

As we age, as technology inexorably overtakes us, as we balance the intimate with the universal, with what might we fill our memory baskets given the extreme fragility of the past? What but stories about ourselves and others by writers who were both like us and unlike us?

—Mini Krishnan
Series Editor

INTRODUCTION

I

THE MODERN ODIA short story is a century and a quarter old; the period from 1898 to 1945 marks the early phase in the development of the genre. It was a time when Odia literature underwent a remarkable transformation, adopting new narrative styles and themes that reflected the shifting social and cultural landscape.

Far-reaching political and social changes were effected by British colonial rule through the use of English as the language of higher learning and governance. This, together with the new employment and occupational opportunities and the rise of industrialism, with rapid mechanization and urbanization, newer and swifter modes of communication and travel, world wars and the struggle for Independence, created what is now called 'colonial modernity'. This impacted the consciousness of writers and demanded that the expansive and digressive oral narration suited to tales and fables told by a garrulous, avuncular narrator be replaced by an authorial presence controlling the economy of the narrative. Writers became increasingly preoccupied with giving voice to the anxiety of coping with a rapidly fluctuating world, which often appeared hostile and incomprehensible.

II

'Rebati', by Fakir Mohan Senapati, was published in the autumn of 1898. A haunting narrative of a young girl's burning desire for learning, it depicts ordinary people and does so in a down-to-earth language spoken in real life. Senapati unshackles Odia from its high-flown Sanskritized version to show that complicated truths underlying the human predicament and the exploration of modern problems, could be expressed in an earthy, everyday prose. The lack of sentimentality, of heavy-handed didacticism and of value judgement makes this story a pioneering work.

While Senapati's characteristic wit and humour, amply demonstrated in 'Patent Medicine'—also included in this volume—is missing here, he makes up for it by using irony instead. The writer, who sent his own daughter to a Christian missionary school, lets his young heroine's wish to study end tragically. Although in favour of women's education, he allows every superstitious fear of the grandmother to come true. It is as if by a literary sleight of hand that the reverse and the obverse of the issue are made to look the same.

Not surprisingly, the story continues to be read and discussed, admired and anthologized to the present day; age has not withered nor custom dulled its appeal.

III

In its day and for decades afterwards, 'Rebati' inspired several fictional forays into the problematic realm of women's education in all its ramifications, including partly Reba Ray's 'The Sanyasi', which has the distinction of being the first modern Odia short story by a woman writer. Published in 1899, less than a year after 'Rebati', Ray's story is only marginally less grim.

However, Senapati's immediate contemporaries were not as skilled and accomplished as he was. Not only did they lack his extraordinary energy and narrative power, but also his dexterous use of the earthy vernacular. Some of the stories produced during the first decade of the twentieth century tended to be what can best be described as 'formulistic' in design. The omnipresent narrator hovered over and peered down at the story's characters and manipulated them more as puppets than as people of flesh and blood. The entire structure was patently conditioned by the author's own predilections—moral, religious, sociological, or political.

It was Fakir Mohan Senapati again who rescued the Odia short story from this arid patch of ten to twelve years. In a rare burst of creativity, he produced four of his memorable stories in one year: 1913. Due to constraints of space, we include only his 'Patent Medicine' here for its takeaway: when all else fails, the broom prevails.

IV

The proliferation of literary monthlies, bimonthlies and quarterlies, to say nothing of the weekly literary supplements of leading

INTRODUCTION

dailies, since the 1910s, inspired a whole generation of writers. These publications, driven by limited space and a desire for variety, encouraged writers to dip into unexplored aspects of the panorama of Odia life.

Since then, the Odia short story has never lacked a fascinated and enthusiastic readership. This could be due to the fact that it remained rooted in tradition while seeking to transform it. By the late 1930s, a diverse group of writers emerged, each contributing to a rich tapestry. While some drew inspiration from folklore and fables, others explored themes of social conflict and injustice, alienation, angst and disillusionment. Their stories captured the evolving aspirations, dilemmas and perspectives of Odia society as they grappled with the challenges of a world undergoing rapid modernization.

A society in flux is bound to reject some of the existing norms, especially those considered outmoded and unjust. Many of the characters of these early short stories are rebels, imbued with a social conscience. But restraint lies at the heart of their rebellion; they question unfair and obsolete diktats of society but never attack its main structures. Nowhere is this more evident than in the relationship between men and women.

The subjugation of women is the theme of many of these early stories. One such is 'A Long Wait', written by a woman writer, Suprabha Kar. Malati, the protagonist, leads a miserable life: a neglected childhood, an alcoholic husband who beats her, the death of her only son; she flees home only to fall into the clutches of a man who pushes her into prostitution. She gets a brief respite when a temple priest gives her shelter, but when her identity is disclosed and the priest loses his job, she puts an end to her life.

INTRODUCTION

Amidst all her trials and tribulations, Malati or her creator never once question societal institutions like the family, nor the well-defined roles of men as the heads of the family, bread-winners and protectors, and that of women as the loving, nurturing caregivers. Indeed, motherhood is highly lauded in this and other stories. It is shown as the acme of a woman's existence, her greatest fulfilment.

Typically, Malati attributes her misfortune to her own ill-fated destiny, not to societal mores. She believes, somehow, that she herself is to blame for her woes. Worse, she feels guilty for believing that her very presence brings bad luck to the ones she loves and thinks the only way out is to drown herself.

As seen from these stories, even the boldest rebel against the established social order is allowed to go only so far and no further. Sulochana in 'Patent Medicine' can give her husband a sound beating but atones for it with fasting and tears. Govind in 'His Better Half' leaves his shrewish wife, but comes back to her after eight years. The sanctity of marriage has to be preserved at all costs, even as Sarada in 'Tiger' protests against her husband's extreme demands. On a lighter note, the eponymous hero of 'Lachhamanji' may chaff against the custom of arranged marriages but is saved by a lucky turn of events when he falls in love with the very same girl chosen by his elders.

If taking one's own life is a form of rebellion against a cruel world, anger against external ills turns inward to destroy characters. Pitei in 'The Witch' does not commit this act of escapism; she simply leaves home, never to be seen again.

Two stories in this collection, 'Bauli' and 'Victory Celebration', offer subtle critiques of government policies. As expected in stories written during the colonial period, their political protest is muted and very indirect.

Not all the stories may be shining examples of flawless craftsmanship, but their hold on the Odia mind has not diminished one bit because of their deep human interest. No wonder quite a few of them found—and still continue to find—their way into anthologies and textbooks.

V

All these writers—with the exception of Senapati, who embarked on his literary career at the ripe old age of fifty-five—began to write in their twenties and thirties and continued to do so for the next three or four decades, in the course of which they each produced a prodigious body of work. The more prolific ones, like Godavarish Mahapatra, Kalindi Charan Panigrahi, Gopinath Mohanty, Rajkishore Patnaik and Surendra Mohanty, published upwards of one hundred stories each—a staggering number, by any reckoning, but even the less productive ones, like Bankanidhi Patnaik, Satchidananda Raut Roy, Rajkishore Ray and Upendra Kishore Das, produced no fewer than fifty each. Nearly all of them wrote in other genres as well. In terms of sheer output, some of these writers were more productive than many of those in succeeding generations.

Output apart, they each developed a distinctive style and voice. Thematically too they tended to be vastly different. True, social realism remained the single biggest paradigm in the early years of the Odia short story, but as life became more complex and its problems more varied and as interactions with international literature and with the literatures of neighbouring linguistic provinces grew, Odia writers began to move away from strictly social themes. They found exploring the recesses of the human mind more challenging and therefore much more interesting; they developed their own voices of storytelling to cope with the new demands of making sense of a transformed society. The world order had changed. Odia authors too reinvented themselves and developed their diction, expression and use of language.

The influence of literature written in English—a language in which all but Fakir Mohan Senapati were educated in school and college—is undeniable, but none of these writers set out to consciously imitate any of those they admired. While they may have absorbed these influences, each developed a unique style.

Some of these writers were at their creative best in and around the same period—between the late 1930s and early 1950s. Many of them also knew one another personally. Some interacted quite regularly at meets and in gatherings, or in one another's homes, where they discussed life and literature in general and sometimes their works-in-progress. These exchanges no doubt enriched their writing; some of these writers remained lifelong friends, but they stuck steadfastly to their different choices of themes as well as narrative voices. Nearly all of them retained their strong bond with the village, but none romanticized rural life; on the contrary, they laid bare its murky world, its yellow underbelly. Stories situated in urban settings were exceptions rather than the rule. Only four stories in this collection—'Australia', 'The Long Wait', 'A House for Rent' and 'Lachhamanji'—are set against the backdrop of the city.

Despite the limited space in this anthology, the selected stories represent the range and diversity of early Odia storytelling. They

INTRODUCTION

offer fascinating glimpses into the lives of characters grappling with social injustices, familial conflicts and personal desires.

Their enduring appeal lies in their ability to transcend time and space, to bridge the gap between the past and present and to speak in the universal voice of human experience. Through the power of storytelling, these writers have captured the essence of Odia society—navigating the complexities of tradition and modernity—and offered insights into the human condition.

In the realm of literary translation, it's often said that one translator is ideal, two are excessive, and three is a crowd. Maybe. But for over a quarter of a century, we—a team comprising an Odia, a Bengali, and a Canadian—have defied this norm, working together seamlessly without a hint of discord. Far from spoiling the broth, our collaboration has made it even more delectable. When asked about our approach, we often invoke the Odia proverb: *pitha khaiba na bindha ganiba*—Would you rather savour the pancake or count the holes in it? If the translation resonates with the reader, does it matter whether one or three translators were involved? As a unit, we've harmonized beautifully, like the three musketeers. Admittedly, our pace is deliberate, and our output isn't prolific, but we weigh every word, ensuring that the soul of the text remains intact and the nuances of the author's work are preserved. As long as we remain true to the spirit—or *prana*—of the text, we feel we have not been the traitors a lot of people out there still believe translators are.

—Leelawati Mohapatra, Paul St-Pierre and K.K. Mohapatra

FAKIR MOHAN SENAPATI

Rebati

(THE FIRST MODERN ODIA SHORT STORY, 1898)

> But oft some shining April morn
> Is darkened in an hour,
> And blackest griefs o'er joyous home,
> Alas! unseen may lower.
> —Rev. J. H. Gurney

'Lo Rebati, lo Rebi, lo nian, lo chuli!'
'Rebati! Rebi! You fire that turns all to ashes.'

PATAPUR—A SLEEPY LITTLE village in Hariharpur subdivision, district of Cuttack. At one end stood Shyambandhu Mohanty's house: two rows of rooms, front and back, with a well in the centre of the inner courtyard, a shed for husking rice behind the house along with a vegetable patch and a garden in front. It was

---

'Rebati-' was first published in 1898 in *Utkal Sahitya*, Vol. 2, No. 10.

in the outer room that visitors and farmers waiting to pay their taxes gathered and made themselves comfortable. Shyambandhu Mohanty, the zamindar's accountant, was responsible for collecting taxes. His salary was two rupees a month, but he could earn a little more by adjusting rent receipts and land records; all told, he earned at least four rupees. With this, he could make ends meet. And not just barely; no, to tell the truth, he was quite comfortable. His family never complained of wanting for anything. They had all that they needed: two drumstick trees in the backyard and a patch of land always full of greens and vegetables, and two cows, which never went dry at the same time, so there was always a little curd and milk in the pails. Shyambandhu's old mother made fuel-cakes from cow dung and husks, so they rarely had to buy firewood. The zamindar had given him three and a half acres of rent-free land to cultivate and it produced just about enough to meet their needs.

Shyambandhu was a straightforward person and the tenants respected, even liked, him. He went from door to door cajoling and coaxing them to pay their taxes; he never demanded a paisa extra from anyone. On his own initiative and without their asking, he would slip four-finger-wide palmleaf receipts into the underside thatch of their houses. He never let the zamindar's muscleman cast his shadow over the village; he'd pump the fellow's palm, fondle his chin, tuck two paise into the folds of his dhoti to buy a plug of tobacco and see him off.

In his own home, Shyambandhu had four stomachs to fill—his own, his wife's, his old mother's and his ten-year-old daughter's. The daughter's name was Rebati. In the evenings, Shyambandhu would sit in his veranda and sing 'Krupasindhu Badan' and other prayer songs; at times he would light an oil lamp, place it on a wooden stand and read aloud passages from the Bhagavata. Rebati always sat next to him, listening with rapt attention. Soon she had learnt a few songs by heart. Her melodious voice lent them more appeal and people would stop by to listen. There was one hymn that gave Shyambandhu the greatest joy and every evening he would unfailingly ask Rebati to sing it:

Whither shall I take my prayers, Lord,
If Thou turnest a blind eye?
Surely shall I be finished.
Be it salvation or damnation,
To Thee this life a dedication,
To Thee, this soul laden.
Empty, empty, all the three worlds
When I am without Thee.
True refreshment, when I thirst,
Only Thy love can be.

Two years earlier, in the course of his visit to the countryside, the deputy inspector of schools had happened to spend a night at Patapur. At the request of the village elders, he had written to the inspector of schools, Orissa Division and an upper-primary school had been established in the village. The government paid the teacher's salary of four rupees a month, to which each student contributed an additional anna.

The teacher, Basudev, a young man of twenty, had attended the teacher-training course at Cuttack Normal School. Urbane and polite, he never took on superior airs. He had been orphaned at an early age and brought up by his uncle. True to his name, he was a fine human being. Charming and handsome—the indelible mark of a bottle's mouth on his forehead applied by his mother to treat diphtheria during childhood enhanced rather than marred his looks. He seemed to have been sculpted out of a single block.

From the time he arrived in the village, Shyambandhu had taken a fancy to him: they belonged to the same caste.

Occasionally, on the day of a full moon or on a Thursday, when cakes and savouries were made at home, Shyambandhu would call at the school: 'Son, come to our place this evening; your aunt has invited you.' A bond of affection had naturally developed between them after these visits. Even Rebati's mother, filled with concern, would sometimes exclaim: 'Ah, the poor orphan! What does he eat, who looks after his meals?' As the visits became regular, with Basu dropping in practically every evening, Rebati would wait at the door to announce his arrival. As soon as she spotted him in the distance, she would call out to her father, 'Here comes Basubhai, here he comes!' Then she would sit beside him and sing all the prayer songs she knew. To Basu's ears, the songs were fresh and ever new.

One day, as they chatted about this and that, Shyambandhu learnt from Basu that there was a school in Cuttack where girls could study and pick up crafts; instantly, the desire to give Rebati an education welled up in his heart. When he confided this to Basu, the young teacher, who had already begun to look upon him as a father, answered: 'I was about to suggest that myself.'

Rebati listened to the conversation and rushed inside. 'I'm going to study,' she announced excitedly to her mother and grandmother. 'I'm going to learn to read.'

Rebati

Her mother smiled. 'Go ahead,' she said, but her grandmother's reaction was sharp: 'What good will it do you? How does book learning help a girl? It's enough to know how to cook, bake, churn butter and make patterns on walls using rice paste.'

That night, when Shyambandhu sat down to dinner on a low wooden stool with Rebati beside him, the old lady sat opposite them, restive and itching to speak her mind: 'Serve him a little more rice, daughter-in-law, give him a second helping of dal and a pinch of salt,' and so on. Then she brought up the topic: 'Shyam, is Rebi going to study? Why should she, son? What good is that for a girl?'

'Never mind, Ma,' said Shyambandhu. 'Let her study if she wants to. Haven't you heard Jhankar Pattanaik's daughters can read the Bhagavata and *Baidehisha Bilasa*?'

Rebati was furious at her grandmother. 'You silly old fool!' she snorted. Turning to her father, she begged him, 'Father, I do want to study.'

'And so you will,' said Shyambandhu.

The matter was left there.

The following afternoon, Basu brought Rebati a copy of Sitanath Babu's *First Lessons*. She was so overjoyed she leafed through the book from cover to cover. The pictures of elephants, houses and cows thrilled her to no end. Kings could be happy to own elephants and horses, others perhaps derived joy from riding them, but for Rebati, it was enough merely to gaze at their pictures. She could hardly wait to show them to her mother and grandmother.

The grandmother did not hide her irritation. 'Take that silly thing away from me,' she shouted.

'Silly you!' the girl retorted.

The auspicious day of Shri Panchami dawned. Rebati took an early bath, put on new clothes and flitted in and out of the house, waiting impatiently for Basu. The usual pomp associated with beginning one's studies was played down out of fear of the grandmother. Six hours into the morning Basu arrived and taught her the alphabet: a, aa, e, ee, u, uu. The lessons went on. Basu never missed a day.

Over the next two years Rebati studied a great deal. All the rhymes of Madhu Rao were on the tip of her tongue and she could reel them off without faltering.

At dinner one night, Shyambandhu asked his mother, as if rounding off a discussion they had been having, 'Well, Ma, what do you think?'

'Nothing could be better, son,' said the old lady. 'But are you certain what his caste is?'

'That's what I was trying to find out. He may be poor, but he comes from a good family. And he's a pucca Karan to boot.'

'Good. Caste counts more than wealth. But will he agree to live with us?'

'Why not? After all, his only relatives are his uncle and aunt. He probably won't insist on living with them.'

What Rebati made of all this she alone knew, but a change certainly came over her. She became noticeably coy with Basu. In the evening she would hang around the front door, as though waiting for someone, which riled her grandmother no end, but when Basu arrived, she would hide inside the house. It took Basu quite an effort to persuade her to emerge for her studies. Blushing and smiling for no apparent reason, she would refuse to read her lessons aloud and would answer him in monosyllables. As soon as the day's lesson was done, she would rush inside, struggling to stifle her giggles.

One Shri Panchami followed another and two years passed. Providence's designs are strange and inscrutable; no two days are alike. One fine Phalgun day, like a bolt out of the blue, a cholera epidemic struck.

Early in the morning the news of Shyambandhu coming down with cholera spread through the village. As always, the immediate response was to bolt the doors and windows and keep out of the path of the demonic deity, as though the evil old hag was out with her basket and broom, sweeping up heads.

Shyambandhu's wife and mother were soon driven out of their minds by worry and anxiety. Rebati ran in and out of the house, crying for help. When the news reached Basu, he hurried from the school and without fear for his own life, sat at the bedside, massaging Shyambandhu's hands and legs, forcing drops of water between his parched lips.

Three hours passed.

Suddenly, Shyambandhu looked up at Basu and stammered: 'Take care of my family, I leave them to you ...'

Basu could not hold back his tears.

Shyambandhu passed away that evening.

The women wailed. Rebati rolled on the floor.

How could the two grief-stricken women and the inexperienced Basu make arrangements for the cremation? Bana Sethi, the village washer man, a veteran of fifty or sixty cremations, saved the day, turning up with a towel around his waist and an axe on his shoulder. Bana was rather philosophical about it: cholera or not, if your time's up you've got to go, whether today or tomorrow, but why miss out on a set of new clothes? Shyambandhu's was the only Karan family in the village and help was neither expected nor forthcoming; the two women and Basudev had to carry the body to the cremation grounds and perform the last rites.

The morning star was shining in the eastern sky by the time they were done. No sooner had they got home than Rebati's mother came down with cholera. By midday, the news of her death had spread through the village.

Providence works in mysterious ways—while one man is blessed with a regal umbrella atop his palanquin, another receives lashes on his fettered hands. Within three months of Shyambandhu's demise, the zamindar expropriated Shyambandhu's cows. Apparently, he had not deposited the last tax collection. This was hard to believe, however. Shyambandhu had always regarded depositing the money as sacred and would not rest in peace until every paisa of the collection was in the zamindar's treasury. The truth was that for a long time the zamindar had had his eyes on the cows. He also took back the three and a half acres he had given Shyambandhu. There was no work for the farmhand and he left on the full moon day of Dola festival. The team of bullocks had already been sold off for seventeen and a half rupees; with what remained after the funeral expenses, the grandmother and Rebati hung on for a month. In the month following these events, they began to pawn household items—a brass bowl one day, a plate the next.

Basu visited them every evening and stayed until bedtime. He offered them money, but they would not touch it. Once or twice, he pressed some on them, but the coins lay idle on the shelf. He had no choice but to accept the couple of paise the old woman produced every eight or ten days to buy them provisions. The house was falling apart, the straw roof had worn thin, but try as he might, Basu couldn't get it re-thatched; the bales of hay he bought with two rupees of his own money rotted in the backyard.

The grandmother no longer cried day and night; she now confined her wailing to the evenings. But she put so much of herself into it that it left her slumped in a heap on the floor for the night. Rebati, convulsing in sobs, would lie down next to her. The old woman's vision had declined and she had a wild look about her. She no longer cried as much and took to heaping curses and abuse on Rebati. The wretched girl was at the root of all her misery and misfortune; her education had caused it all—first her son had died, then her daughter-in-law; the bullocks had been sold off; the farmhand had left; the cows had been taken by the zamindar; and now her eyes had gone bad. Rebati was the evil eye, the she-devil, the ill-omened.

The moment the curses started coming thick and fast, Rebati would shrink from her grandmother and hide in a corner of the house or the backyard, tears streaming down her cheeks.

The grandmother held Basu equally to blame. If he had not been so eager to teach the girl, she could not possibly have gone and taught herself! But the grandmother could not take Basu to task, because she couldn't do without him. The zamindar kept seeking flimsy clarifications and almost every second day, a messenger came asking for this account or that. Basu alone could fish them out from the clutter of papers Shyambandhu had left behind. Yet, behind Basu's back, the old woman sometimes gave vent to her feelings.

Rebati's presence no longer filled the house; gone were the days when she would be heard mourning loudly. Nobody heard her voice, nobody saw her out of doors. Her large brooding eyes, awash with silent tears, looked like blue lilies floating in water. Her heart and mind broken, day and night were alike to her. The sun brought her no light, the night no darkness; the world was an aching void. The memories of her parents overwhelmed her, their faces hung before her glazed eyes. She could not bring herself to believe they were truly dead and gone. Hunger no longer stirred her stomach; slumber no longer closed her eyes. She went through the pretence of eating only out of fear of her grandmother; she grew thin and emaciated, her skin hung loose on her bones and she could barely lift herself off the floor where she lay day and night. The only time she revived a little was when Basu visited them. She would sit up and fasten her gaze on him, lowering her eyes with a sigh when their eyes met. But the next moment she'd feverishly stare at him again. For those brief hours of the day when he was around, Basu completely possessed her eyes, her mind and her heart.

Roughly five months had passed. On a hot Jaistha Saturday afternoon, Basu knocked on their door. Never before had he ever called at such an unusual hour. The old woman was full of foreboding as she let him in.

'Grandmother,' said Basu. 'The deputy inspector of schools will be camping at the Hariharpur police station and giving the students an oral test. All the schools have been informed; I received the order today. Tomorrow morning, I'll have to start off and be away for about five days.'

Listening to the conversation from behind the door, Rebati felt her legs give way. Her hold on the door was barely tight enough to stop herself from falling.

Basu bought them enough rice, oil, salt and vegetables for five days and bade them goodbye.

'Son,' said the old woman with a sigh. 'Don't walk about in the sun for too long. Take care of yourself; eat your meals on time.'

Rebati could not take her eyes off him. Before, she would look away when their eyes met, but today she stared unblinkingly, unabashedly into his eyes. A change seemed to have come over Basu too. For a long time, he had contented himself with stolen glances, but today he did not turn away. They stared deeply into each other's eyes.

Evening came; darkness filled the house and covered the earth. Rebati remained rooted to the ground until her grandmother's piercing screams jolted her to her senses. Basu had left much earlier.

Rebati counted the days.

On the morning of the sixth, she even rushed a couple of times to the front door, which she had avoided since her parents' death. Six hours had passed when the schoolboys arrived from Hariharpur, bringing the news of Basu's death. He had succumbed to cholera under the big banyan tree near Gopalpur on his return journey. The village mourned; the women and children shed copious tears.

'What a handsome fellow!' said one.

'So polite,' said another. 'Never hurt a fly,' remarked yet another.

The grandmother cried so much she choked. 'Poor boy!' she repeated between sobs. 'You only brought it on yourself!' Implying that he had perished in his prime because he had been foolish enough to want to teach Rebati.

Rebati sank to the floor and lay there without a whine or a whimper.

The grandmother woke up the following morning without Rebati beside her and shouted out in anger: 'Rebati! Rebi! You fire that turns all to ashes.' She worked herself into a fine froth and passersby heard these terrible words repeated all morning long.

Half-blind and angry, she groped her way through the entire house. When she finally found the girl, she was shocked. Rebati, burning with fever, was unconscious. Worry and fear gnawed at the old woman's heart. She couldn't decide what to do, whom to turn to for help. Exasperated, out of breath and without hope, she tartly commented: 'What medicine can there be for an illness of one's own making!' Rebati had brought the fever on herself by daring to study.

One, two, three, four, five days passed. Rebati remained glued to the ground, her eyes and lips shut. On the sixth morning, she let out a whimper or two. The old woman ran her hand over the girl's body. It was cool to the touch; perhaps the fever had left. She called out to her and Rebati mumbled a reply, then asked for water, stared around wildly and broke into incoherent babble. One quick look and even a country doctor could have quoted from his text: 'Thirst, fever, delirium; of imminent collapse these are the symptoms.' But the poor grandmother was overcome with a sense of relief. The fever had left; the girl was able to open her eyes and speak two words, to ask for water. A little gruel was all she needed to regain her strength and get back on her feet.

'Don't get up,' the grandmother said. 'Stay where you are. I'm going to cook you a bit of food.' She left the room and rummaged in vain among the earthen pots for a handful of rice. Her head became clouded with despair and she sat down with a sigh. If only her eyesight had been better, she would have realized the provisions meant for five days had already lasted for ten.

But there was a flicker of hope in her yet. She picked up the only object of value left—an old brass bowl with a hole in the bottom—and set out for Hari Sa's store. The so-called store was in Hari's residence, in the middle of the village and he kept a paltry stock of rice, salt, lentils and oil to sell to travellers passing by.

Hari saw the old woman with the bowl. He understood immediately but let her first make her plea. He then took the bowl and examined it minutely, turning it from side to side. 'There's no rice,' he said, handing it back. 'Who's going to give you anything for a bowl like this?' Of course, he had both rice and the inclination to sell it, but getting the brass bowl for a song was what interested him the most. The grandmother staggered at his words, as though lightning had hit her. What would she do if she didn't get any rice, what would she cook for Rebati, how would the girl fight her weakness? She sat there for hours, depressed and silent, still as a log, casting imploring glances at the shopkeeper.

The day wore on. Realizing she had left the sick girl alone for a long time, fear stirred her old heart. 'Time I got back home,' she mumbled to herself, picking up the bowl. 'God knows how that girl of mine is doing.'

'Never mind,' said Hari grudgingly. 'Give me the bowl. Let's see if I can scrape up a little something for you.' He gave her four measures of rice, half a measure of lentils and a handful of salt. The old woman hobbled back home, resting every four steps or so to catch her breath. She hadn't even washed her face since morning and her mind was in a whirl.

She reached home hoping Rebati was better. She thought she'd ask the girl to draw water from the well. The rice wouldn't take long to cook.

She called out to Rebati once, twice, three times, but got no response. Then she yelled at the top of her voice: 'Rebati! Rebi! You fire that turns all to ashes.'

By now Rebati was sinking fast. Her body, already feeble from spasms of excruciating pain, had turned ice-cold. Her thirst was so terrible that she felt as if her tongue was being sucked back into her throat. She found the room unbearably hot and crawled out to the inner courtyard. Even that brought no relief. She rolled out to the veranda at the back and propped herself up against the wall.

Dusk had fallen and a gentle breeze was blowing. A bunch of bananas hung from the tree her father had planted before his death. The guava sapling her mother had planted two years ago had grown to a considerable height and was covered with blossoms. Rebati remembered how she had drawn water from the well in a small jug and tended it. This brought back a rush of memories of her mother. Her head was in a whirl, her thoughts jumbled, but the image of her mother clung to her.

Night slowly descended. Darkness stole out from the boughs of the trees and shrouded the garden. Rebati tilted her head back and watched the sky. The lone evening star was gleaming brightly. She could not take her eyes off it; and it grew and grew and grew, bigger and brighter, invading the whole sky and behold! Her loving mother sat in the heart of it, her face glowing with love and kindness, her arms extended towards Rebati in invitation. Rebati was overwhelmed. Two shafts of light pierced her eyes and moved down to her heart. Her breathing, heavy and laboured, rose and fell, breaking the stillness of the night. She wheezed, choked and cried out to her mother twice.

Then there was silence.

The grandmother crawled around the house, going from the living room to the courtyard to the rice-husking shed, but Rebati was nowhere to be found. Then it occurred to the old woman that with the fever abating, the girl might be taking a stroll in the garden at the back.

'Rebati!' she screamed. 'Rebi! You fire that turns all to ashes.'

She crawled out to the narrow veranda, which was only one hand wide and two high and bumped into the girl. 'Death to you!' she cried. 'Sitting here, are you?' She wanted to shake her up, but she could sense something was amiss.

She ran her hand over the length of the girl's body and then held a finger close to her nostrils. The night's silence was rent by her eerie wail. Two bodies fell from the veranda and thudded to the ground.

That was the end of Shyambandhu Mohanty's family.

The last words that had emanated from his house were: *'Rebati! Rebi! You fire that turns all to ashes.'*

REBA RAY

The Sanyasi

(THE FIRST MODERN ODIA SHORT STORY BY
A WOMAN WRITER, 1899)

I

A DESTITUTE WOMAN HAD recently taken shelter in Nityananda Patnaik's home in Jajpur, along with her six-year-old daughter. The widow of a zamindar, she was from the same caste as Nityananda. Three years earlier her husband had lost everything in a lawsuit and consumed by the pangs of poverty, had chosen not to continue among the living. Those three years had been a harrowing time for her. Finally, when she had nowhere else to go, Nityananda had offered her and her daughter, Parasamani, a place in his house.

Nityananda had worked in the treasury office in Cuttack and was now on a pension. He had also inherited a small zamindari and lived quite comfortably. His was a small family—wife, Ushabati and son, Shiva Prasad. An only child, Shiva Prasad had been

---

'Sanyasi' was first published in 1899 in *Utkal Sahitya*, Vol. 3, No. 6.

The Sanyasi

born after prayers to Lord Shiva over many years and so it was appropriate he should have been named after the God. When the boy was thirteen, Nityananda had sent him off to stay with a friend in Cuttack, so he could get a decent education.

Nityananda's wife, Ushabati, was as proud, foul-mouthed and haughty as her husband was gentle, calm and collected. After moving in, Parasamani's mother attended to every chore around the house, but no amount of slaving seemed to satisfy Ushabati. On the contrary, the poor woman was frequently subjected to and singed by the raging flames of the mistress's anger. Even little Parasamani was not spared; she too had to put up with slaps, blows and pinches. God Almighty be praised that He has bestowed on the lowly and downtrodden enormous reserves of patience! What would have happened to these poor souls if they had lacked forbearance? It was just as well that Parasamani's mother took every bit of humiliation without demur. Nityananda was blissfully unaware of all this—not that he would have been able to do a thing about it had he known.

Shiva Prasad was delighted to have Parasamani around when he came home for Durga Puja. As a single child, he had been lonely for as long as he could remember. He was a quiet and kind boy, which made it easier for Parasamani to take to him.

One day, sitting beside Shiva Prasad while he was studying, she blurted out—perhaps out of childish enthusiasm or from deep-seated desire—that she, too, wished to study.

Shiva Prasad found a copy of *Barna Bodhak*—a primer—right away and began teaching her. Until he left for Cuttack at the end of the holidays, he guided her through her lessons every afternoon, encouraging her to read and to write the alphabet and words with chalk. In just about twenty days, Parasamani mastered nearly half of *Barna Bodhak*. But her studies were interrupted when Shiva Prasad returned to Cuttack.

Six months passed. Shiva Prasad was back home for the summer vacation. Parasamani's studies resumed and after finishing *Barna Bodhak*, she started on *Bodhadayak*. One day, Ushabati chanced upon her son teaching the girl and hurled uncalled-for abuse at them. From then on, Parasamani did not seek Shiva Prasad out; she studied by herself.

The girl grew up to be an unparalleled beauty, graceful and well mannered; everyone took to her at first sight. Nityananda never missed an opportunity to express his love and affection for her. Perhaps because he did not have a daughter of his own, or because he was naturally generous of heart, or because Parasamani's sweet innocent face was difficult to resist. But unfortunately, the girl failed to gain even the smallest place in Ushabati's heart.

II

Five years went by, with days good and bad, all ultimately drowned in the boundless depths of Time. Many, dragged out of dark despair, reached the blinding illumination of happiness, while others, deprived of joy, were submerged in a bottomless ocean of grief. Who could count the number of human beings Time sent—against their wishes—to their deaths, just as it showered blessings on a grieving world by bringing forth a bountiful crop of babies, as lovely as fresh flowers?

But, through good fortune or bad, not much changed in Nityananda's family. Among the good things, Shiva Prasad passed his Intermediate Arts examination and returned home. Ushabati's fond wish now was to get her son married and she began to pester her husband about it day in and day out.

One day, Nityananda took her aside. 'Place your hand on my head and swear you'll not refuse my request.' She hesitated but let herself be persuaded.

'When Parasamani was just two years old,' Nityananda confessed, 'I met her father on some business. One look at the child and I thought to myself: God willing, someday I'll get our son Shiva Prasad married to her. So intense was my wish that I let her father in on it and we both swore we'd not let it be otherwise, even if one of us were dead.'

It was as if Ushabati had been struck by lightning. 'Is that why you asked me to place my hand on your head and swear? What will people say if I accept Parasamani as my daughter-in-law? Aren't there other beautiful girls around? How can I settle for a girl whose mother doesn't have a coin to offer as dowry? You want me to give my son in marriage to a girl whose mother works as a servant in this house?' Protesting vehemently, she trotted out more arguments.

Nityananda listened in silence. 'I cannot go back on my word,' he said quietly. 'If you're unwilling, you may do as you wish. But you'll be on your own when it comes to your son's marriage.'

For the next eight or ten days, husband and wife did not talk to each other. Ushabati vented all her anger on Parasamani and her mother, who in the meanwhile had come to know of what had transpired.

In the end, with no other solution in sight, Ushabati gave in.

On an auspicious day and at an auspicious hour, the holy union between Shiva Prasad and Parasamani was solemnized. Nityananda was euphoric that he had been able to keep his word. Parasamani's mother was ecstatic that the best possible match had been found for her adorable daughter. The only person who was unhappy was Ushabati. What about the newlyweds—did they feel blessed and happy to have found each other?

III

After the wedding, Nityananda did not let Shiva Prasad return to Cuttack to continue his studies despite the boy's fondest wishes. Shiva Prasad also tried, not once but two or three times, to look for a job, but had to give up the idea because of his father's opposition. No one knew what arguments Nityananda marshalled in support of his stand.

Ushabati was an ill-tempered person by nature and her ire against Parasamani increased after she became her daughter-in-law. Parasamani's slightest lapse provoked disproportionate outbursts. Ushabati could not get over her old habit of raising a hand to the girl. Once, Parasamani, dead tired, let her eyes close for a few seconds while preparing the evening meal and, instead of meting out the regulation beating, the solicitous mother-in-law simply poured a pitcher of cold water over her.

Parasamani's mother learnt to keep quiet even as she witnessed her daughter's misery. And Parasamani herself remained as silent as a deaf-mute, drowning her sorrows in her mother's affection and her husband's love. At the tender age of fourteen, she worked untiringly from dawn to two hours past dusk, attending to chores of all kinds, but in great fear of her mother-in-law's curses and beatings. The few words of love and solace she received from her

The Sanyasi

husband before she offered herself up to a restful slumber at the end of the day made her feel like the luckiest woman alive.

His mother's ill treatment of Parasamani did not escape Shiva Prasad. Although he could not say a word to his mother, one day he said to his wife: 'I know how miserable and tormented you are, but it is my loving request to you not to take Mother's unkind words to heart.'

'How can one who has your love be bothered about anything?' Parasamani replied. 'Besides, sometimes I do make mistakes and deserve what comes to me.'

One day, Parasamani came down with a fever. She lay in bed in her mother's room. When, after five or six days, the fever showed no sign of abating, Nityananda called in a vaidya, who took her pulse and wrote out a prescription. Ushabati didn't step inside the room even once to see how her daughter-in-law was doing. Parasamani's mother used the short breaks between her own chores in the household to drop in to give her daughter some food—toasted rice flakes, ginger, salt and pureed puffed rice. Without telling his mother, Shiva Prasad too went some three or four times to see his wife. After Parasamani recovered, Ushabati confronted her son about it. God knows what she said, but Shiva Prasad felt deeply wounded.

Five or six days later, he begged his father to let him visit Cuttack, saying how much he missed the town and how badly he needed to see it one more time. Nityananda finally agreed, but only to a short visit. An auspicious time for the boy's departure was decided: between the coming Tuesday night and dawn on Wednesday.

On the night before he was to leave, Shiva Prasad begged his wife to take care of her health. She was with child. Husband and wife held each other a long time, crying silently. When morning came, Shiva Prasad took leave of his parents and others and started on his journey.

He put up with a friend in Cuttack and wrote to his father within a fortnight, giving him the good news that he had landed a job with a monthly salary of fifty rupees. He took it and was in no hurry to return home. This was exactly what a doctor would have prescribed an ailing man.

Four months after Shiva Prasad left home, Parasamani gave birth to a baby boy. Nityananda promptly wrote to Shiva Prasad with the happy news. But his family was not destined to enjoy this joy and happiness for long: the newborn deserted his mother's lap while she was still confined to the labour room and returned to the fairyland whence he had come, plunging the entire family into grief. Parasamani came down with a fever almost immediately, from which there was no remission for the next fifteen days.

When he received the sad news, Shiva Prasad wanted to visit home but could not, since he did not want to apply for leave from the job he had only recently taken.

Nityananda called in country doctors and proper doctors to treat his daughter-in-law, but to no avail.

One day, quite secretly and with a lot of difficulty, Parasamani wrote her husband a letter.

Dearest,
Your poor one wants to see you once before breathing her last.

The Sanyasi

Will you be kind enough to take the trouble of coming here and helping your servant fulfil her last wish—to take the dust from your feet on her head before dying?
Forever yours,
Parasamani

She entrusted the letter to her mother, asking her to place it in an envelope with a postage stamp and find a trustworthy woman to take it to the post office. Parasamani's letter moved Shiva Prasad so deeply that he requested a week's leave and rushed home.

It was as if the flickering flame of Parasamani's life had been waiting for one last glimpse of her husband's face. For once, Shiva Prasad, past caring about his mother's feelings, went straight to his wife the moment he reached home. The poor girl burst into convulsive sobs when she saw him.

She beckoned him to approach. When he did, she took his right hand and clamped it to her heart. 'How I had looked forward to placing your son in your lap! Not only did my wish not come true, it will remain forever unfulfilled. This is the last time we'll meet in this life and I pray to God that I may have you as my husband in my next.'

It took an enormous effort for Parasamani to speak these few words. Tears silently streamed from Shiva Prasad's eyes and drenched his wife's hands. Parasamani's mother rushed to her daughter's bedside, crying bitterly. Hearing her, Nityananda and Ushabati too rushed in. Parasamani requested each of them to bless her with the dust from their feet. Then she looked at her husband longingly one last time and took her last breath.

Two months went by, with yet another bereavement: Parasamani's mother, grieving over the death of her only child, followed her into the other world. Was all this predestined, ordained by God? Could anyone have changed any of it?

Shiva Prasad did not go back to Cuttack. He withdrew from everyone, keeping to himself. His parents wanted him to remarry.

In a short time, a suitable match was found. The girl was a rich man's daughter and Ushabati, elated, saw this as the fulfilment of her true wishes—all the wishes that had eluded her when Shiva Prasad had married Parasamani. Soon preparations were afoot for an early wedding the following month.

Parasamani might have died but Shiva Prasad constantly felt her presence. She was always around, gently laughing, extending her hands towards him, begging for his love and affection. So when he learnt of the plans for his second marriage, he did not hesitate for a moment to tell his mother straight out: 'I'm not going to marry again. Don't you people even think of it.'

His mother was stunned, as if felled by a blow. 'Son, even men in their dotage get married two or three times. You're a young man, yet you refuse to remarry? What will happen to us if you don't? We'll simply perish.' She used all sorts of arguments—some harsh, some sweet.

But Shiva Prasad was unmoved. 'I won't marry again.'

When the matter reached Nityananda's ears, he thought that these words had come from his son's lips, not his heart and that the boy would come to terms with it once the marriage took place.

The wedding day dawned. It was already eight in the morning, but there was no sign that Shiva Prasad had woken up. Wondering why, someone went to his room. Not finding him there, he combed the whole house. When Nityananda was finally informed, he too started looking for his son in every nook and cranny and sent out search teams. Ushabati's tears of joy soon turned into tears of grief and anguish.

The people sent out to search all returned dejected. A joyous and festive day darkened into one of agony and despair.

Nityananda and Ushabati cursed and cried themselves hoarse. The light had gone out of their home.

Though Shiva Prasad had expressed his unwillingness in no uncertain terms, he knew his parents would overrule him and go ahead with the second wedding. So, on the night before the wedding, after everyone had gone to bed, he put together a few clothes and a little money and secretly left home. Undecided where to go, he first headed for Cuttack. But he didn't feel comfortable going there, aware his father would soon get wind of where he was. So he decided to go to Calcutta and felt somewhat relieved when he reached there. Not immense, unalloyed relief, but relief nevertheless. His more immediate worry was how to face the future.

A month passed. His money ran out. He had not cultivated the acquaintance of anyone in the city who could help him out with a loan of ten or fifteen rupees to tide him over.

One day, tormented by worries and anxiety, his hands clasped across his heavy heart, he was sitting in his room when he overheard someone singing in the next room. He was so drawn to the music he went next door and sat beside the singer, plying him with requests to continue.

The last song was one of renunciation and non-attachment. It touched Shiva Prasad to the core, changing his life in that instant.

The song was like a beacon, showing him the direction his life should take.

The next morning, Shiva Prasad donned the robes of a mendicant and repeated the holy names of the Almighty; the All-Merciful; the Lord of eternal happiness, love, kindness and peace; the Great Father; the Eternal One. Seeking shelter in Him, he set out to roam the wide world and sing His praise.

It is difficult to explain to readers the great peace and joy that came over Shiva Prasad, who did nothing but speak of God, at whose feet he had found refuge. He had at last installed God in his heart, to whose mercy creation owed all its limitless splendour and riches.

Epilogue

Our wish is not to bring the story to a close with the sad plight of Nityananda and Ushabati. But for all those curious to learn the couple's fate, here it is.

Shortly after Shiva Prasad vanished, Ushabati died. Nityananda sold off his property and keeping just a little for his upkeep, made an endowment for the temple services of Lord Jagannath. He moved to Puri, where he did not live for long; he soon left for the divine abode.

FAKIR MOHAN SENAPATI

Patent Medicine

Forget about going out in the evenings, he wasn't to leave the house even during the day—she'd given him strict orders. 'Whatever you want to do, do it at home—read, write, whatever. Don't let me catch you anywhere else.' Only after the poor man had begged on bended knee had Sulochana relented a bit and allowed him a brief morning stroll in front of the house. But on no account was he to wander out of sight, even by accident. 'If you do, there'll be hell to pay. Remember, I'm going to keep an eye on you from behind the door.'

Early one morning, as Chandramani was out walking, he saw a boy beckoning to him slyly from a distance. He blinked and rubbed his eyes: why, wasn't he that smart boy from Bhadrak! His heart fluttered with excitement. He motioned to him to come closer and, glancing furtively towards the door, inched towards him.

'Patent Medicine' was first published in 1913 in *Utkal Sahitya*, Vol. 17, No. 6.

they met, he turned his back to the boy, all the while nervously watching the house. Cautiously, he extended his left hand behind him. The boy thrust a piece of paper into it, turned and ran away. Chandramani kept a tight grasp on the paper and walked back towards his house. Once he was sure his wife wasn't watching, he hurried through the letter, tore it to pieces and scattered them to the wind.

A little while later, he went inside and called out lovingly to his wife: 'Can you hear me, dearest? Can you come here for a second, please?'

'My, my, what politeness!' his wife answered testily. 'What have I done to deserve that? Must be my lucky day. What do you want to tell me, anyway?'

'Just that for the last four days I've been in agony. My head keeps spinning all through the night, my stomach aches and I get pins and needles all over my body.'

'What's this—another trick? You've brought this suffering on yourself. Remember all the ganja, liquor and all the other awful things you've consumed! See, what such abuse has done to you. You've contracted all the diseases in the world. One after another three jobs came your way, but you couldn't hold down even one of them. I don't mind you losing the jobs, I don't mind you losing money—whatever had to happen, has happened. All I want now is that you should get well. For the last four months, I've watched you like a hawk, making sure you stayed off liquor and ganja and your health is showing signs of improvement. But now you seem to be itching to get back to your old ways.'

'Come, come, my dear. It's not that. I met Madhavacharya a little while ago. The old astrologer worked out the position of my stars: Scorpio and Cancer are in unfavourable positions and Saturn is clearly hostile. It's the stars that are making me suffer so much. So why not have a little puja performed to appease them?'

'Is that what the astrologer advised?'

'Yes, and he said I should visit all the Shiva temples in Bhubaneswar, Khandagiri and Udayagiri, with enough money to pay the priests to pour a hundred—no, a thousand, that's it, a good thousand—pitchers of water on the image of Lord Shiva. Then the stars will be mollified and my misfortunes over. I'll soon recover my health and never again be tempted to use intoxicants.'

A slight suspicion crossed Sulochana's mind. 'Did the astrologer come to the house?' she demanded to know. 'How come no one told me!'

'Oh, no . . . The astrologer himself didn't come. Only his son.'

'Since when does he have a son?'

'Oh, no, no,' Chandramani stammered weakly. 'His servant.'

Sulochana scrutinized her husband's face; she knew he was lying through his teeth. All he wanted was to get sozzled with his drunkard friends and carouse with the whores in Telenga Bazaar. What hadn't she tried to get him to mend his ways! Let him out of her sight for a moment and he'd slip back into his dirty old habits.

'You're going nowhere,' she said firmly. 'You're staying home.'

'You're right, quite right. Three days is quite a long time to spend away from home. I think I'll make a short trip to the temple of Lord Dhabaleswar. I'll start out now and come back by evening.'

'No, you're not going anywhere.'

'All right, give me a few rupees. I'll just go and offer worship at the Shiva temples in town.'

'Fine, tell Makra to get a buggy. We'll go together.'

Chandramani turned away with a sigh. He gave the matter a little thought. A bright idea came to him; he almost congratulated himself aloud.

'Listen,' he said animatedly. 'I'm hardly in a state to go around to different places; doing so will only worsen my illness. In fact, there's no need for that at all. The astrologer said I don't need to go out anywhere; it's enough if I meditate on Lord Shiva at home.'

'What kind of meditation?'

'I'll have to lie face down, on the floor, with a blanket over me for five full hours—from now to nine in the evening. I'll meditate on God and think of nothing else.'

'Will that appease the stars?'

'Oh yes, according to the astrologer, it certainly will. He said something else as well: I have to pledge ten rupees to Lord Shiva and put the money under my head when I begin the meditation. After a month, when I'm well, we'll offer worship to Him and feed some Brahmins and Vaishnavs with the money.'

'Won't you eat anything today?'

'Ram! Ram! Does anyone have food while meditating on God? I'll fast the whole day; I won't touch even a drop of water.'

'As you wish.' His wife heaved a sigh. 'Go get started.'

'One more thing,' Chandramani added, confidence returning to his voice. 'Meditation can't be performed here; the surroundings have to be suitable. You've often cooked fish and meat here and the smell has polluted the place. My prayers today aren't to just any ordinary deity; they're to Lord Shiva and Goddess Parvati. The small front room in the outer wing is a bit less polluted and quiet too. But remember, if the shadow of a woman falls on that room or if I hear a female voice, my meditation will be ruined.

Everything will come to nought! Make sure no woman comes anywhere near the room.'

Sulochana went into the inner wing of the house, depressed, thinking about the ordeal in store for her husband. When the Brahmin cook asked her what dishes he should cook, she snapped, 'Your master's fasting. How can I eat anything? No cooking today.'

The old cook went away, smiling to himself. What a strange lady the mistress was. When the master was even slightly indisposed, she'd nurse him day and night and forget to have her meals. But when she lost her temper, she'd rush at him with whatever she could find—a stick, a broom, or whatever—and abuse him using the vilest possible language.

Her temper was short and her tongue razor sharp. Yet, all said and done, she was a good soul. A rich man's daughter and a rich man's daughter-in-law, she had a big heart.

Chandramani called Makra, the servant boy, to the outer wing of the house and spoke to him in whispers: 'Makru, my boy, listen. You'll do something for me, won't you? Go and lie down in the front room, covering yourself with this blanket. I'll be back in the evening. Stay there until then. Don't leave the room for any reason at all.'

'No, master,' Makra protested. 'I can't do that. If the mistress finds out, she'll be very annoyed with me.'

'You rogue, you rascal, you devil! How dare you disobey? I'll give you a good thrashing.' But softening immediately, he added, 'No, Makru, no. I was only joking. Listen to me; you want to visit your uncle in Kendrapara, don't you? You can leave tomorrow morning. I'm giving you four days off. Here, take these four rupees and have a good time. I'll also buy you a shirt tomorrow.'

Makra needed no further encouragement. He lay down in the room and pulled the blanket over himself.

Sulochana was feeling low. After a bath, she spread a mat out in the bedroom and sat down to pray to all the Gods and Goddesses she could think of. 'O Goddess Kali of Kaligali! Restore my husband to good health. I pledge you two black saris and will sacrifice two black goats.' Lord Dhabalaeswar too was promised a thousand panchamritas.

The prayers went on and three long hours passed. Sulochana began to worry about what her husband would eat when he had finished meditating. Cooked food was out of the question; he would only have fruit. So she laid out a meal of bananas, coconut, cheese, curd and milk.

She looked out and saw the lengthening shadows and realized that the day was nearly done; the sunlight had retreated to the rooftops. With no chores to do, she paced restlessly about the house.

As evening fell, she cautiously went near the front room. She remembered her husband's warning that no woman should cast her shadow there and made sure that didn't happen. She stuffed the end of her sari into her mouth, lest a word escape her lips and pushed the door ajar.

The room was dark. Her husband lay absolutely still, meditating. How he must be suffering! O Gods, let him be cured of his addictions! Let him give up all intoxicants! Goddess Kali, I promise I'll sacrifice a black goat and a black rooster.

She knelt and touched the ground with her forehead several times in supplication. She pushed open the door a little more and tiptoed into the room, her foot landing on her husband's head. She quickly bit her tongue and jumped back. 'What have I done, oh what have I done! What a sin!' She burst into tears. With folded hands she silently prayed for forgiveness from her husband and the Gods. Then she carefully picked her way across the room and touched his feet three times with her forehead. The blanket seemed to shake violently.

'Alas! Alas!' Sulochana muttered to herself. 'He's dripping with sweat!' With the end of her sari she tenderly wiped his feet and back. But she was in for a shock when she came to his face: her husband's moustache was missing! What could have happened? She felt for it two or three times, but it simply wasn't there. Growing suspicious, she flung the blanket back. What she discovered made her jump back and scream in fury: 'You vile wretch, you scum, you vermin, you Makra, why are you lying here?'

What could poor Makra say? With folded hands, he stood silently against the wall, trembling like a thief.

Sulochana raved and ranted.

The shouting and screaming wore her out after a while and she realized they wouldn't help.

She had to get to the bottom of this. Makra had to be won over. 'Makru!' she said endearingly. 'You want to visit your uncle, don't you? Leave tomorrow. Take four rupees to cover your expenses and sweets. Tomorrow, I'll buy you a pair of Maniabandhi dhotis you can wear. Don't breathe a word to anyone. Go sit quietly in a corner in the kitchen.'

Makra had expected a good hiding from her, but what was this—he was being given four rupees and promised a pair of dhotis! He was overjoyed. He took out the four rupees his master had given him and added it to what he had received just now, counting the money: one, two, three times, before tucking it carefully into the waist of his dhoti. Then he went and hid in a corner in the kitchen. Sulochana lay down in his place on the floor.

Three hours into the evening, Chandramani stumbled back into the house. He was completely drunk, his feet unsteady and his speech slurred. He threw the door open, saw Makra lying on the floor and felt so relieved that he broke into a song and dance: 'What damned good fun—the kick of liquor and opium! Get up, Makru, my brother! Well done, my Makru! Makrum, my mate, get up, get up. Who's afraid of any bastard or bitch? What fun I've had today, how can I ever put it into words? Your mistress—no better than a maidservant—had me on a tight leash for four long months. My mouth had dried up. But in one single day with that wonderful woman of mine I've had all the excitement I'd missed for months! Have I told you about her? Our affair started three years ago, when she came to dance at Gopal Babu's place. She's terrific! Do you know her name? Imagine: your mistress is called Sulochana; *sulo* grows in ponds and *chuna* is used for making cakes. What a disgraceful name! But my darling's name is Us-man-ta-ra. How beautiful! May you live long, my Usmantara! Her nature is as sweet as her name is lovely. See, Makrum, see how nice and considerate she is—she doesn't forget old flames. She sent for me the moment she set foot in Cuttack yesterday. When I saw her this afternoon, oh brother, I felt I had got my treasure back. She too was so happy that her face lit up. A feast of ganja and liquor began as soon as I sat on her mattress. Everything had been laid out in advance: crushed ganja buds, opium hookah and liquor. First, the liquor bottles were opened. Not your ordinary Aska rum, it was the original number one English stuff. If you could guzzle just a glass of that rum, you'd know what it is. The two of us emptied the bottle in no time. We drank it neat, mind you, without a drop of water. Your mistress daily prepares puree, sarabhaji, khiri. What terrible food! Fit only for cats. But Usmantara, she gave me fried gram and crispy roasted fish. They go so well with rum! I greedily filled my belly. Remember how I tricked your mistress and wheedled ten rupees out of her? Does anyone ever go to these pleasure dens empty-handed? Usmantara turned her face away when I placed the money before her. But I'm not a fool like your mistress; I'm one clever man, you know. I could sense that Usmantara found it too paltry a sum to accept. How could she have accepted it, she who makes hundreds of rupees a day? When I told her I'd be back with a hundred rupees tomorrow, she laughed and said, "Do I care for money? It's just you I want!" Very true, does she really care for my money? All she wants is pleasure and fun. Money means little to her, she has plenty of it. But I'll keep my word and give her one hundred rupees. The word of a man and the tusk of an elephant are the same: both unbreakable! Do you know where I'll get these hundred rupees? Ha, ha! Your mistress has kept the land revenue collection safely stashed away in a chest. I'll jimmy it open with an iron rod. I've already done this a couple of times. Neither your mistress, nor her father, nor even her grandfather will get an inkling of it. There's a lot of money in that chest. If I could get it all, I could drown a big chunk of Cuttack town in a tide of liquor and fun! If only your damned mistress would drink a glass of liquor, she could get to know this world of pleasure! What a pity! Only Usmantara knows this world. Your mistress—hell, she's a wooden puppet. What delicious eats I've had with my drinks today! Your mistress' father—that bastard—couldn't have tasted such stuff in seven lives.'

Sulochana sprang up, tossing the blanket aside. 'What did you say?' she roared. 'What did you say, you drunkard? May witches devour you! Since when is my father a bastard? Where have you been the whole day, you rascal, and who's this Usmantara?'

'No, no. I didn't go anywhere,' he stammered, frozen with fear. 'I just went out for a pee. I can touch your head and swear it.'

'You liar,' his wife exploded. 'How dare you touch my head? You want me to drop dead?'

She picked up a broom from the floor and started beating him with it. The blows fell on his head, his back, his hands, just about everywhere. Chandramani couldn't bear the pain. He tried to run away but tottered and fell. Her blows rained down on him.

When Sulochana was exhausted, she went into the inner wing and slumped to the floor. She broke down and prayed helplessly: 'O God, forgive me. Lead my husband back to the path of virtue.'

The night passed.

The next morning Sulochana found her husband lying sprawled out in the dining room. The effects of the liquor had worn off; the cool morning breeze had made him drop into a deep sleep and he was snoring. She could see that the broom had left marks all over his body; blood had clotted in some of the bruises. 'What have I done!' she cried disconsolately. 'I beat my husband with a broom! What terrible fate will be mine?' She prayed to the Gods again and again, begging their forgiveness, tears streaming down her face. She brought a bowl of linseed oil and gently rubbed the swellings.

Chandramani woke up, opened his eyes a crack and found his wife sitting beside him. He panicked: who knew, she might give him another beating! He lay deathly still, his eyes shut. A little later, he looked furtively at her face and saw no trace of anger. Her eyes were flooded with tears and she was tenderly rubbing oil on his legs.

Sulochana could see that her husband had woken up. She sent for four pitchers of water, helped him sit up and gave him a nice bath, which soothed the burning sensation left by the beating. While she bathed him, he sat as motionless as an idol, dead sober. She made him change into dry clothes and pressed him to eat. Then she lovingly tucked him into bed. She herself hadn't eaten anything since the day before. She wept incessantly, praying the Gods to forgive her sin.

Throughout the day, neither husband nor wife exchanged a word. The servants too remained silent. Wracked with guilt, the couple felt embarrassed to look into each other's eyes and wondered how to make up. Chandramani vowed to himself that from then on, he would consider all intoxicants as repulsive as excreta or cow's blood.

Six months rolled by. Neighbours, relatives and friends noticed how unusually quiet and peaceful Chandramani's house had become. He and his wife no longer quarreled; just the opposite— they were always together, chatting happily and reading books. They started subscribing to magazines and journals like *Utkal Sahitya*, *Mukura* and *Dipika*. In the past, Chandramani had borrowed large sums of money against promissory notes and now more than half his debt had been paid off. He didn't stir out of the house, even if his wife tried to force him to. He would even turn down invitations to plays and dances. Occasionally in the evening, husband and wife took a buggy and went round the town.

The whole town was amazed. What had happened? People recalled that Chandramani's father, Shyam Pattanayak, a rich zamindar, had engaged private tutors for his son, who had also attended an English medium school. But what had come of all that study? He had fallen into bad company and become an addict. His mind brimmed over with nasty thoughts; he lost his character, frequented disreputable places and went around with drunkards and bad elements. A few well-wishers had suggested that perhaps marriage would change him for the better. The zamindar had then taken the beautiful and accomplished Sulochana, the only daughter of Ram Krishna Mohanty, as his daughter-in-law. But even after this, his son had not mended his ways. He continued to steal money from home and squander it. He thought nothing of signing promissory notes for sums far in excess of what he had actually borrowed. Neither his home nor the zamindari concerned him in the least. The old zamindar realized that at this rate his worthless son would blow his fortune, so he had willed everything to his daughter-in-law. But neither his father's will nor his father-in-law's attempts at persuasion had had any effect on Chandramani. So what had happened now to make him a reformed man? Gopi, the town wit, wisecracked: 'The change came about because of the sound thrashing he got from his sweet little wife. The broom seems to be the best medicine for diseases like addiction and debauchery.'

'How come this medicine isn't prescribed by either the Indian or the foreign system of medicine?' asked Shyamaghana, cracking up.

'Don't you understand?' said Gopi. 'This is the mistress's own invention—her own patent medicine!'

LAKSHMIKANTA MAHAPATRA

The Old Bangle-Seller

It was a fiercely hot day in the month of Phalgun. The sun beat remorselessly down on the village road where the old bangle-seller was walking, a basket on his head. He was perhaps nearing sixty, or maybe even older and was as toothless as a newborn. Silvery white hair covered his chest and head. Drenched in perspiration, he trudged along.

At the edge of the village, he stopped by the big house. It had a high veranda, plastered with cement; the straw thatch over the roof was perched high, thick and in seven tiers; the front doorway was massive. The old man gently eased his load down and waited to catch his breath.

After a while, a maid sauntered out and noticed the old man. He was someone she knew.

'Budha Shankhari' was first published in 1914 in *Mukura*, Vol. 8, No. 11.

'There you are, bangle-seller, after a pretty long time,' she said with a smile. 'Have you got anything new?'

'Of course,' said the old man. 'But daughter, first get me some water. My throat is dry and I'm dying of thirst. Oh, this heat! It'll kill me.'

The maid fetched a big jug, which the old man eagerly lifted to his lips. He poured the water down his throat, half-emptying it at one go. 'Bless you, daughter,' he said with a profound sigh. 'God bless you.'

'Enough, enough!' The maid giggled. 'Come inside. My young mistress wants to see your bangles.'

The old man rose to his feet, picked up his basket and followed her inside.

They went past the main entrance and the hallway, through the enormous, paved courtyard with a cemented platform in the middle, to reach the spacious living quarters at the rear. The young daughter-in-law of the house, the end of her sari over her face, stood at the door. The old man lowered his basket and waited.

'Go on,' the chirpy maid prompted the young lady. 'Ask him to show you his wares. Don't feel shy, little mistress. Come, come, he's an old man. Why don't you rummage through his basket yourself?'

The young mistress pulled back her veil and stepped forward with a smile. The old man looked up at her and was mesmerized by her beauty. Her face was like a sculpture and radiant like a champak flower. The red silk sari she wore down to her ankles revealed her svelte figure. The old man's eyes, lit with joy, riveted on her face. His eyes feasted on her and he wanted to recite his sales pitch, but for once couldn't find the words.

The Old Bangle-Seller

It took him a while to get a grip on himself. 'Choose anything you like, Mother,' he said. He didn't know why he had addressed her as 'Mother' but then he had felt a world of good. His heart suddenly brimmed over with happiness.

'You have Asman Tara bangles?' the young woman asked, overcoming her shyness.

The old man could not recollect having ever heard a sweeter voice; it was like liquid honey. Her words rang in his ears long after she had spoken.

'No, Mother,' he said. 'But there are many other varieties—Rangajhiliri, Baulaphulia, Bichhamalia, Chunatipi. Pick out anything that takes your fancy. I will get you Asman Tara bangles as soon as I can.'

The young woman selected some bangles, but she wondered if they would fit.

'Come, Mother,' said the old man. 'Give me your wrist and I'll try them on you.'

The young woman hesitated.

'So shy, Mother?' The old man laughed. 'And of me? Am I not your old son, huh? Do mothers feel shy with their children?'

The perky maid gave a hoot of laughter. 'What luck, young mistress! What a wonderful old son to have, I say!'

'Oh, away with you!' the young mistress giggled, holding out her wrists to the old bangle-seller.

What beautiful hands, the old man thought. Soft, plump, pink, full of life and good fortune; the long tapering fingers could put champak buds to shame. Were they ordinary mortal hands or chiselled and honed to perfection by some celestial craftsman? How could he touch them, hold them in his own harsh, callused and dirty paws? His hands trembled when he finally took her left palm and gently squeezed it to slip a bangle on. Her wrist was so fragile and delicate that the bangles looked earthy and crude; a little carelessness on his part and she could be hurt. With wrists like these, he had to be gentle as never before.

As long as her hand was in his, his happiness was boundless. There had been no greater bliss than this in all his sixty-odd years on earth and nothing certainly half as soul-satisfying. If only he had wrists like these to slip bangles onto every day of his life!

Just then her mother-in-law emerged from the living quarters and the daughter-in-law, hurriedly drawing the veil over her face, scampered off. The old mistress looked at the maid. 'Buying bangles, are we?'

'Yes,' the maid replied. 'The young mistress wanted to have some.'

The old lady turned to the bangle-seller. 'What do they cost?'

'Cost?' said the old man. 'How much can a few bangles cost?'

'Tell me how much so that I'll pay for them.'

'Nothing. I'll not accept a paisa from Mother.'

The old lady, a shade surprised, turned to the maid. 'What's this Mother business about?'

The maid giggled. 'The old man has made himself a son of our young mistress.'

The mother-in-law gave a tiny flicker of a smile. 'All right, old son, accept the price of the bangles this time. Next time you may give away some for free. You're a poor bangle-seller, after all.'

'It's my gift to Mother. Sorry, I can't accept money for them. A few bangles will make me no poorer than I already am.' He smiled, picked up his basket, hoisted it on his head and hurried

The Old Bangle-Seller

out of the house. The maid ran after him for some distance, calling for him to stop and take the money, but the old bangle-seller did not look back.

So moved was the old man that from then on, he unfailingly visited the village every second or third day. But bangles were not something people bought daily; women wanted them only once in a while and especially during the festivals. Still, he would religiously go from door to door, hawking his wares. Sales didn't matter, he wasn't really keen on his business. All he longed for was a glimpse of his little Mother. He would not stop at the outer door of her house but march right into the courtyard. 'Does anyone here want new bangles?' he would trill out, not bothering to lower his basket and wherever the young woman was, she would bustle out happily and stop by the door. The old man would take a long look at her face, his heart overflowing with ecstasy, half-hoping she would say yes so that he'd have an opportunity to hold her divine hands in his again and slip bangles on them. But the young woman would smile and shake her head and the old man would slowly leave with a sigh. Sometimes when the old man called, the young mistress was a little slow in showing up, then the perky maid would pitch in: 'Young mistress, where are you? Look, your old son's here!' Then the old man too would cry out with professional flair: 'Bangles! New bangles! Wonderful bangles!' The daughter-in-law would appear with an amused grin.

This had come to be a routine and every time the old man came to see her, he vowed to himself that he must make a bunch of Asman Tara bangles as soon as he could. The Rajo festival was not far off and would be a fitting occasion to change old bangles for new. She would hold out her lovely wrists to him and how he would take them, one after the other, in his own and slip the bangles on! The mere anticipation could keep him buoyed up for days, even for weeks and months. He couldn't wait for Rajo to arrive.

Meanwhile, it was the month of Baisakh and the heat was unbearable. As old and feeble as he was, the bangle-seller could no longer withstand the strain of his visits to the village. He fell ill and ran a high fever for several days, his legs and hands swelled and the way he clung to bed, his neighbours wondered whether he would pull through. But the old man himself wasn't in the least bothered; his only worry was that he had not seen his little Mother for a long time. He could hardly bear the torture.

The Rajo festival was now just a few days away. Two long months had passed since the bangle-seller had last seen the young woman. If he had been able to stand up on his legs, he would surely have dragged himself all the way to her house. But then how could he go and see her without the promised bangles? It was high time he stirred himself, collected the ingredients and made some Asman Tara bangles. True, it was still quite painful for the old man to sit up, but he wouldn't dream of having somebody else do the work. So, he got down to it himself, summoning every bit of his fifty years' experience of bangle-making; and certainly, he did not mind if the usual one day's work took all of four; the bangles simply had to be matchless, out of this world. And that's how it went. The bangles were finally finished just two days shy of Rajo. They were perfect, just as he had dreamt; he had never made anything half as beautiful before. He was thrilled. How lovely these would look on his Mother's delicious wrists!

The Old Bangle-Seller

Rajo was now only two days away. The old man had not slept a wink the previous night. The girls and young women would put on new clothes and new bangles first thing the following morning. 'What shall I do?' he thought, despair tugging at his heart. 'I can't walk a step and I wouldn't dream of sending her the bangles through someone else. I haven't seen her for ages. My days are numbered; and if I don't see her now, perhaps I never will. Never will I have another occasion to hold her hands.' He found inexplicable strength surging through his tired, weary, feeble limbs.

Next morning, he had an early meal, carefully wrapped the bangles in the end of his towel, hung it gently across his shoulder and set out. Every step was torture and the distance of ten miles took him inordinately long; it was well into late afternoon when he reached the village.

He stopped at the same spot in the courtyard where he always had and called out, his voice breaking with joy and happiness: 'New bangles! Little Mother, come on out. You wanted Asman Tara bangles, remember? I've got them for you.'

But no one came out and no one answered.

'Little Mother!' the old man raised his voice. 'I've got lovely bangles for you.'

The old lady of the house came out, with the maid in tow.

'Where's Mother?' asked the bangle-seller. 'I've got Asman Tara bangles for her. She'll wear them for the Rajo festival.'

The maid who had always laughed and joked with him in the past remained solemn and silent.

The old lady gave the old man a cold look. 'Nobody in this house will ever need new bangles,' she said curtly.

'Don't say that!' cried the old bangle-seller. 'I've made these for my little Mother with so much love and care.'

'She needs them no more.'

'All right, forget the bangles. Call her out and I'll just see her once and leave. I haven't seen her for ages.'

'You can't see her.'

'Can't see her?' The old man felt a bolt of lightning striking his head. His eyes instantly welled up with tears. 'But why? Please, please, I want to see her. Just once. You can see I'm going to die soon.'

The old lady turned to the maid with a frown. 'Go tell the daughter-in-law.'

The maid left.

After a little while, the young woman came silently to the door and stood exactly where she always did whenever he called. She did not have her tinkling ankle-bells and instead of her beautiful red silk sari with golden borders, she wore a plain white cotton sari.

A tremor ran through the old bangle-seller's body. His head swam and his eyes closed, smarting with tears. He looked up at her again, this time searchingly at her wrists. Those lovely hands were bare, without bangles. He burst into a wail.

The young widow silently withdrew.

'Little Mother!' lamented the old man, choking in grief. 'Mother!' He unwrapped his towel, took out the bangles he had fashioned with so much love and care and dashed them in the courtyard. They broke into smithereens. Then he turned and left without a backward glance.

After he was out of earshot, the old lady and the maid burst into heart-rending sobs.

GODAVARISH MISHRA

His Better Half

Govind, twenty-two and bread-winner of the family, had married four or five years ago. Once married, people usually become rather anxious to have children, but not Govind. A lower-division clerk in the Collectorate, he was not too well-off, but he tried to make do with his meagre salary. Clerks tended to make something on the side, but not Govind.

No one knew why he was always so morose, the pallor stemming from some deep regret and mortification, clouding his face. He never went straight home from the office, choosing instead to hang out by himself, avoiding friends, acquaintances and neighbours. For hours on end, he sat on the riverbank or by the side of a pond, lost in thought. A casual glance was enough to realize he was being consumed not only by hunger but by something else. The sight of him moving about aimlessly led to the belief there was no spot where he could find peace of mind.

'Srimati' was first published in 1914 in *Utkal Sahitya*, Vol. 18, No. 1.

He almost shunned his house. He went home only for meals, which he took in the sitting room—where plates of food were left for him. There were days when there was no food at all. On those occasions, the poor man got by on an empty stomach, not just the whole day but the whole night too.

Sarat, once his classmate in college, was now a deputy magistrate and Govind's boss. Govind had to go to him for instructions, carrying files himself. Many of his classmates had become deputy magistrates, lawyers, professors, public figures; a few had given up on lucrative careers to devote themselves to the cause of the country. Govind's regret was that he remained on the lowest rung. There was simply no improvement in his career. 'Why?' he'd wonder, plunging into endless thought. 'What went wrong?' None of his expectations had materialized. He would sigh long and deep, his eyes swimming.

His better half was just a little over eighteen. Besides her, there was only a maid to attend to the household chores. (He thought of himself as a servant too. After all, what else was he?) Just three mouths to feed, but still his salary of twenty-five rupees a month was inadequate to make ends meet. That had fuelled his wife's annoyance. She was always angry, irritable and in a bad mood. She had endless complaints: the household expenses far exceeded his salary; she hadn't received a single new piece of jewellery since her wedding; the smoke from the clay oven in the kitchen not only blackened her clothes but also hurt her eyes; living in a mud house had darkened her fair complexion. 'Why am I not dead and gone?' she'd moan loudly enough to be heard. 'Did *he* not know when we got married that I am a deputy magistrate's daughter and that we are zamindars too? A husband who can't keep his wife in some comfort! Why should such a man decide to marry at all? Why try to reach for the moon when you can't even touch the top of your own head?'

But why on earth should one pay any attention to an angry wife's harangues, when all sorts of people in and out of home bombard one with lectures of all kinds? Because this young wife was not just anybody. She was educated, knew three languages—Odia, English and a bit of Bengali—and she also read, including every single detective or romance novel! Her greatest complaint was that while she was exiled to her husband's house, she couldn't afford to buy a single book to relieve her boredom. It was only when she made a trip to her parents' that she had a chance to loll in bed, read and drown the sorrows of a life doomed to poverty and want.

Her parents' happy home was overflowing with all the luxuries she craved, but like most married women, she didn't like to remain ensconced there for too long. (Of course, it was quite another matter whether she'd have been allowed to, even if she had so wished.) Besides, here she couldn't indulge her newly acquired habit of constant sniveling and badgering. Even a hoarder can make do without money, an illiterate without an education, an artist without poetry or music, but a woman who'd discovered her voice can't do without hectoring and badgering. So it was with the young wife; she missed scolding and lecturing so much she'd leave the comforts of her parents' home and rush back to her husband's.

Once when she returned from her parents, she ran smack into her husband in the sitting room. They hadn't met face to face in a long time. Govind always did his best to avoid her; he simply had no stomach for it. He had taken to spending time outside the home, either on the riverbank or at the edge of a pond—places he had grown very fond of.

The exchanges between the two touched a new low: the broom saw its debut. Govind's shrivelled body and soul smarted under the strokes on his back.

It was during this historic evening that he bade farewell to his home, to the street outside it, to the pond and the riverbank, to his office and set off aimlessly. Little did he know that he had embarked on a new phase of life.

Left alone, the wife soon began to be haunted by memories of her husband; his absence began to tell on her nerves. The little nest egg—nothing much really, just a month's salary—he had left behind was depleted in just ten or twelve days. So she had no choice but to move back with her parents. But things did not go too well there. Her skill at bitching and haranguing—honed to perfection at her husband's and which had become second nature to her—did not endear her to anyone. Soon enough she made the place too hot for anyone's comfort. The maids and servants all revolted and on their recommendation—which her parents tacitly endorsed—it was decided she must move back in with her husband. So in the end she had no choice. For the first few months, provisions had been supplied by her parents, but then they began to dwindle, in quantity as well as quality.

Thus it came to pass that the young woman who had always dreamt of a life of ease and comfort, of being given whatever luxuries took her fancy, who had wanted her life to go off like a song, was in for hard knocks and quite a few of them, at that. With her wishes dashed and hopes withered, her life turned into hell. She, who used to fly into a towering rage because she couldn't make do with twenty-five rupees a month, now had to depend on the pitiful dole from her father. She, who had hated the mud floor of her husband's home, which she complained had coarsened and darkened her skin, now made her peace with the crumbling walls, with no repairs in sight. She got reconciled to living in dirt and squalor. She no longer complained about the soot from the oven blackening her sari, because the oven went unlit for days on end.

She took to visiting the riverbank, the ponds and the wells—places her husband had once frequented. She had no one to whom she could talk about how meaningless her life was. For days on end, she lay enclosed by the crumbling walls of the house, worrying where the next meal was coming from. She slowly realized she was missing her husband, that her life could be saved only by him and not by her parents or their wealth. Where was he? Would he ever come back? Was he alive at all? Oh, where was he?

After roaming all over, Govind reached Kanpur, a city well known for its leather industry. There, impressed by his abilities, the manager of a shoe company offered him employment. But even as he threw himself heart and soul into the new line of work, he never ceased thinking about his wife. She might have behaved badly, but she was still his wedded wife. And young too, still in her teens. How was she faring? Awake or asleep, he worried about her; misgivings plagued him.

In just about two years, Govind learnt the ins and outs of the shoe trade. The manager became a close friend too. One day, while telling him the story of his life, he spoke of his wife: 'My father-in-law was born in a poor family, but he grabbed the opportunities that came his way and got himself a decent education, which helped him land a plum government job. His salary as a deputy magistrate was handsome, but he made much more on the side and accumulated enough wealth to buy a zamindari. He lured me into marrying his only daughter with the solemn promise of financing my education, but after a few months, he reneged on that and stopped all help. So I had to drop out of college and look for employment. The job I found wasn't exactly a godsend, but with my qualifications I could expect nothing better. The salary was low and my wife constantly complained that she couldn't make ends meet. Things got so bad that I left. Poor dear, what's she doing now, how's she faring!' Govind was in tears.

The kindly manager packed him off to Young Shoe Company in Calcutta with a glowing letter of recommendation. The company had fallen on bad days due to poor management and Govind was taken on as the new manager on a monthly salary of five hundred rupees. In next to no time, Govind made a name for himself in the trade circle; he revived the fortunes of the company. The shoes manufactured by the company were of such high quality that buyers no longer bought from Utkal Tannery. There was a rumour that even Madhu babu was ready to poach him for his Chauliaganj factory, on a princely salary of one thousand rupees a month.

Even in the midst of all this, Govind did not cease thinking about his wife. He sent her money orders for three hundred rupees from the very first month of his employment. He kept this up without fail.

Next door to Young Shoe Company, where Govind worked, was the premises of Long Company, a wine merchant. The postman often mixed up the mail for the two and many a letter addressed to Long Company landed in the mailbox of Young Shoe Company. Govind found among these letters cheques sent by his father-in-

His Better Half

law to the wine merchant, sometimes for very large sums of four or five hundred rupees. Despite all that had happened in the past, he sent every letter and cheque next door.

The despairing wife gave up all hope of ever seeing her husband again. She didn't lack for anything, but she no longer needed so much money. What she was in acute need of was something money or gold and silver couldn't buy. So she started giving her money away to charities; there were so many needy and poor people around. She continued to live in the same old crumbling house—keeping the meagre flame of hope burning in her heart.

Meanwhile her father fell on bad days, his zamindari was auctioned off, the mansion in which he lived was sold, his pension was put on hold. Matters came to such a pass that in the end the old man didn't know where to turn; he and his wife were out on the street. Like all the poor beggars in the town, he too came to hear of Govind's wife and her charity. At the same time, however, he remembered how uncharitable and unkind he had been to her after she was abandoned by her husband. He remembered how he had treated poor Govind like a dog too—not only had he let him down after making solemn promises, but he had also abused him every step of the way. All these memories assailed the old man's mind, as he battled the twin disasters—remorse for his heartlessness and pangs of hunger.

Govind too was not at peace, although he sent money to his wife every month without fail. He had deserted her for now nearly eight years—not a small stretch of time by any reckoning. How was she faring in his absence, how was she managing? A deep longing to see her constantly gnawed at his heart. Then, one day, he received a letter from her. A short letter, just two lines: 'You are sending me more money than I can spend. I shall consider my life fulfilled if you let me have just a glimpse of you. Your wife.'

The wife's parents had finally moved in with her and she spent much of her time taking care of them. The days were long and dreary, but she doggedly kept at her chores to escape the pangs of an all-consuming hope of her husband's return. She had never cared for anyone in the world, but now with her parents around, she discovered the daughter she should have been all along. Whenever they now addressed her as 'daughter', she thought of the past with deep nostalgia. But more than anything, she longed to get someone else back in her life, someone who mattered more than anyone else.

At long last, Govind quit Young Shoe Company and returned home. Eight long years had gone by. He stopped at the riverbank, by the edge of the pond, at the side of the road; from a distance he could see his crumbling house.

The joy of the reunion of husband and wife cannot be described in words.

Govind remembered all his childhood friends—Gopal, Madhu, Mohan, Anand and the rest. They had been to school together. They had all given up great careers to work for the future of the country. He had always admired them. Now he was about to follow in their footsteps; now he knew he had his work cut out for himself. It had to be something in which the well-being of his wife would be paramount. The income might not be much, but it would be enough for a family of four—his better half, her parents and himself—to get by.

BANKANIDHI PATNAIK

Lachhamanji

'Do you ever think beyond your own meals and your office?' Balaram's wife began complaining that morning. 'Do you even notice I'm ready to drop dead from worry, so why on earth would you?'

'What's the matter?' Balaram took the pipe out of his mouth. 'What are you going on about?'

'Nothing, nothing. Why should *you* worry about such trifles! It's all right for *you* to slouch back in the reclining chair with a book or newspaper, day or night. *You* don't have to bother about what's happening at home.'

Balaram smiled. 'Tell me, is it laid down in the scriptures that women can't blow off steam without a long-winded preface? Or is it some holy man's curse that makes you behave this way?'

'Lachhamanji' was first published in 1915 in *Utkal Sahitya*, Vol. 19, No. 2.

'Go on, blame everything on women. The fault is all theirs. After creating man, God must have lumped together whatever was left over and from that created woman, so she'd be forever subservient to man; be his life-long slave; suffer the humiliation, insults and pain heaped on her by him as his legitimate right. She must cry until the stream of tears reaches down to her toes. She must carry a girl in her womb for ten months, but not speak a word about her future and welfare. Never mind. Why should I worry myself to death? It's now entirely up to you; it's your headache to find a match for her. Surely nobody's going to blame me if the girl remains unmarried. But as a mother, how can I be indifferent to all that?'

'Whose marriage are you talking about, our Mali's?'

'Who else's, yours? Did you think I was nagging you to take a second wife?'

'But that's not a bad idea at all. After all, I'm not over the hill yet. The flesh may seem a little weak, but the spirit still is willing.'

His wife was in no mood for the banter. 'Do as you please,' she said, stomping off highly annoyed. 'Never again will I bring up this topic.'

Balaram had already started thinking. The smoke curling up from his pipe vanished in the air. He hurriedly dashed off a few letters to some of his close relatives, urging them to immediately look for a suitable match.

A few days later, on an official tour to Bankipur, he was out on an evening stroll along the bank of the Ganga. A beautiful spot. The river musically flowed past in a happy hurry, the trees on the bank shimmering in the mellow sunshine, when he was startled to overhear snatches of a conversation in Odia. How sweet the voices sounded, how heart-warming the words! Listening to his mother tongue spoken outside his home state, the words and sounds of his own language overwhelmed him.

He turned back to notice a young gentleman in conversation with someone who was obviously from the working class. The young gentleman was speaking fluent and flawless Odia, but from his clothes and manners, he didn't look like he was from Odisha.

'Sir,' Balaram couldn't help asking. 'Are you an Odia?'

'Yes, I am. And you, sir?'

'Oh, it seems we both are from the same state. Are you working here?'

'Yes sir, I'm a sub-deputy collector.'

'Since when?'

'Recently, and I am still on probation. But I lived in Patna for years.'

'Why there?'

'I lived with my parents and studied there. My father worked in Patna. When he passed away, I had to settle my mother and sisters in Odisha, but went back to Patna to look after our properties and also to complete my education. As soon as I graduated, I landed this job.'

'May I know your father's name?'

'Gopinath Das.'

'What! And which part of Odisha are you from?'

'Kalyanpur, Cuttack district.'

'Then you must be Laxmidhar Das, aren't you?' Balaram couldn't suppress his surprise.

'How do you know, sir?'

Balaram spluttered with joy. 'How? Well, well, Gopi was a close friend of mine; we went to school and college together. When he moved away to Patna we fell out of touch. You might not remember—how could you, you were just a toddler then—but I bounced you on my knees and you played with my son Hari.'

Laxmidhar was taken aback. 'Sorry sir, I'm unable to place you.'

'You must know Bhatapada, the village next to yours, don't you? Well, I'm from there and my name is Balaram Mohanty. I work and live in Gaya and I've come here on official work at the local court.'

'I've heard of you from my father, sir,' the young man said politely. 'You are the zamindar of Bhatapada, aren't you, sir?'

'That's right. I'm currently the first munsif in Gaya. But tell me, who looks after your affairs in Odisha when you live and work here?'

'My uncle, sir. Fortunately, he belongs to my village. Since my father's passing, he's the head of our family. Without his help and support I'd have stopped my studies and working here now would have remained a distant dream.'

'And what's your uncle's name?'

'Mayadhar Das. He's the head clerk in the collector's office.'

'Oh, Mayadhar's your uncle? Why, he's a very good man. He'd never neglect you.' A short pause. 'Are you married and all?'

Laxmidhar felt a little shy and his head drooped. 'No, sir.'

'Why not?'

'It's all up to my uncle, sir.'

Another pause. 'And where are you staying here?'

'With Surendra babu. May I invite you to lunch at our place tomorrow, sir? I'll come to fetch you in the morning.'

Lachhamanji

'Unfortunately, I'm leaving by the evening train. Never mind. The thing is I'm so happy to have made your acquaintance, young man. Come to think of it, you and I are quite close. So I'll make it a point to put up with you when I'm here next time. Now I must hurry if I'm to catch my train.'

Such a good-looking young man, Balaram kept thinking as he took the train back to Gaya. And so polite and well-mannered too. He'd make an excellent match for my Mali. God willing, the two might be joined in holy matrimony yet. Maybe that's what is written in their stars.

When Mayadhar received Balaram's letter, he thought to himself: No wonder our young Laxmidhar, educated and well-placed, is considered such a prize catch. It'll do no good to delay his marriage any longer; besides, no better proposal might come our way. Balaram Mohanty's pedigree is impeccable. He's well-known and his daughter is not only pretty but educated and well-bred too. In the past, the Mohantys had been uppity and looked down their noses when it came to striking matrimonial alliances with what they considered lesser families like ours. All angles considered, an opportunity like this should by no means be missed, no, not by a long stretch. And Laxmidhar—he's so obedient he'll not dare to go against my wishes. But still, he ought to be consulted. After all, he's educated and of the modern generation.

With these thoughts in mind, he dashed off a letter to Laxmidhar, emphasizing more than once that this match was not only desirable but unmissable. But when it came to replying to Balaram's letter, he was in a bit of dither: What should he write? After all, he, Mayadhar, represented the groom, the side of the wedding party with the most influence and it wouldn't reflect well on him to seem too eager or desperate. So putting a lid on his excitement, Mayadhar sent a brief but polite message that although personally he wasn't averse to the proposal, he couldn't commit himself before consulting Laxmidhar.

When he received his uncle's letter, Laxmidhar wasn't exactly thrilled. But in order not to offend the old man, he wrote back:

Respected Uncle,
I reside forever at your lotus feet. Your letter is self-explanatory. You needn't have bothered to elicit my opinion on the matter in question. Your wish is my command. However, since you've always wished me well, I'm sure you'll not hurry in this matter and you'll think through it all, to do only what's best for me. I'm a bit rushed at the moment, caught up with office work, but I hope to write again soon.
Forever yours obediently...

Laxmidhar's reply put Mayadhar at ease and he wrote to Balaram the same day welcoming the match. After the wedding date was finalized, he informed Laxmidhar that the wedding, which everyone in the family was eagerly looking forward to, was fixed for 23 January, the seventh day of the bright fortnight of the month of Magh, and as the bridegroom, he, Laxmidhar, should reach the village at least fifteen days in advance.

Laxmidhar hadn't remotely expected that the matter would be concluded so swiftly and that his uncle would take no notice of the strong hesitation on his part. In a quandary, not knowing how to react or what reply to send his uncle, he decided to consult his childhood friend Binod. He wrote:

Lachhamanji

Brother, you may have heard that my marriage with Balaram Mohanty's daughter has been fixed. I don't know whether to be happy or sad; my uncle's letter has left me sort of catatonic. Balaram Mohanty might be a well-respected person in the whole of Odisha and being married to his daughter might push me up a rung on the social ladder, but I've no idea what the girl is like. I don't know the first thing about her—her character, her values and views. I don't even know what she looks like. Marriage is a big decision, an unbreakable union for life. You can well understand how far from desirable it is to marry a girl not seen with your own eyes but through somebody else's. Don't for a moment think I'm advocating the kind of pre-nuptial courtship practised in the West, but neither am I in favour of an arranged marriage based purely on social, familial and material considerations. The girl might be a paragon of virtue and a great beauty to boot—in which case it's a piece of great good luck—but then again, she might be the exact opposite. In any case, marriage is too important an issue to be left entirely in somebody else's hands, to somebody else's judgement. So brother, it's my earnest request that you check on the antecedents of the girl and fill me in. You know how much I rely on your judgement. My future is now in your hands. I can't speak about it with anyone in my family and neither should you. I'm not saying that our guardians aren't our well-wishers, or that they're out to deliberately make our lives miserable, but they should spare young men their misgivings by eliciting their views and opinions on a matter as important as marriage. Don't think I'll be at peace after writing to you. I'm trying to go home and do a bit of digging on my own too. There's still some time—two months is a long time, long enough to make or mar one's life. Once again, don't breathe a word of this to anyone. Hope you're doing well.

Affectionately yours . . .

Laxmidhar was somewhat relieved after he had mailed the letter, but not much; his mental peace was already in shreds.

The wedding was only a month away and Balaram knew he wouldn't get a long spell of leave. So he instructed his son, Hari, 'You must leave with your mother, Mali and the others right away. I'll join you in the village some ten or fifteen days before the wedding. There's plenty to do, arrangements to oversee, invitations to send out; it pays to get a head start. None of the pre-wedding ceremonies need be skipped nor delayed. If you don't reach the village well in advance, your poor brother Govind will be hard put.'

The idea appealed to everyone and the first convenient Sunday was fixed for the journey. But Balaram's wife, who suffered from colic, came down with a severe attack on the morning of their departure, so it wasn't prudent to let her undertake a long train journey. 'She can stay,' Balaram said. 'I'll bring her with me. But Mali must go. True, her mother's presence would have helped a lot, but what can be done when she's so unwell?'

Hari took the train with his wife and sister as decided. They got into a second-class compartment that had only one other passenger, a young Hindustani man. After Hari had hauled their luggage aboard, stacked and arranged it properly, found his wife and sister their berths, he lighted a cigarette and was about to strike up a conversation with the co-passenger, when he noticed all of a sudden that his pouch was missing. He turned the compartment upside down looking for it, but it was nowhere to be found.

Wondering whether he might have left it in the waiting room, he jumped out and dashed off. The first bell had already been sounded and not more than a couple of minutes were left before the train started. Then the second bell rang. People were running on the platform; the din was so great one couldn't hear oneself speak. Mali and Hema looked out the window with mounting anxiety, but Hari was nowhere to be seen. Soon the crowd thinned and with a shrill whistle the train shuddered and began to chug out of the station. Desperate but faint wails issued from the lips of the two women, but they didn't carry far. They became more and more frantic by the second, but they didn't know what to do, how to deal with the crisis. The greater their anxiety, the greater their helplessness. They had never faced anything of this kind, having been raised like delicate potted plants. Not only was there no man to accompany them, they considered the co-passenger more as a threat than a help. At their wit's end, they could see nothing but darkness, thick darkness, all around. It was as if a terrible monster had abducted them and was spiriting them away to the nether world.

Noticing their agitation, the Hindustani young man tried his best to calm them down, but the more he tried the more their tension grew. So in the end he fell silent and sat back quietly.

After a long while, when their agitation seemed to have ebbed a little, he tried once again to draw them out. In half-Bengali and half-Hindi, he wanted to know who they were, where they were headed, why they were travelling. The answers he received were hesitant, reluctant, monosyllabic, mechanical.

Meanwhile, the two women's suspicion deepened. They were hit by misgivings: Why was the fellow plying them with so many questions if he didn't have some evil designs up his sleeve? Brought up on chilling stories of railroad mishaps and crimes, they found it hard to imagine that under the hard exterior of a Hindi-speaking upcountry man, there could be a kind and sympathetic heart. Any gesture or behaviour on the man's part that served to entrench their prejudice, they accepted as the gospel truth; whatever seemed to go in his favour, they rejected out of hand.

After they had recovered a little more, they began to take stock of their situation. The first thing they did was to discreetly take off their gold ornaments, put them into little bundles and tie them to the ends of their sari. The sight of all that gold, who knew, might whip up the young man's greed and lust.

The young man couldn't help smiling to himself. Whenever the train stopped at the bigger stations, he asked them if they needed food or water or anything, but the women remained resolutely silent. On their part, they thought only the devil could be so solicitous and sweet-tongued. They remained awake and watchful, clinging to each other. To put them at ease, the young man pretended to sink into a deep sleep, but he was beginning to worry about them.

When they reached Gomo, where they had to change trains, the two women refused to budge, no matter how much he reasoned with them. They thought the fellow was up to something. But when they found the whole train emptying, they got down and let the young man engage a coolie to shift their luggage to the connecting train.

After the night passed and morning came, they felt their fear receding. Unbidden, the young man fetched water so they could wash their faces, brush their teeth; he got them breakfast. He behaved exactly as a close relative would. Maybe even Hari himself wouldn't have been half as caring and attentive. And yet the fellow wasn't being over familiar and fawning; everything he did seemed so natural, nothing obtrusive, nothing out of the way.

In the face of his faultless decency, their misgivings fully crumbled; once the ice of suspicion had melted, the two women felt irresistibly drawn to him. From then on, they began to notice only signs of good breeding and nobility in every little action and word of his: Could such unselfish and well-behaved young men still be around? Look, we don't know him at all, but how concerned he's been about our safety and security! He's neglected even his own comfort while looking after ours. What'd have happened to us if God hadn't brought him to us? What a shame we were so suspicious and distrustful of him.

'Truth to tell,' Mali confided to her sister-in-law, 'I didn't harbour any suspicion. I thought to myself that someone as handsome as he could never be vile.'

Hema gave a low chuckle. 'My, are we already so taken up with his good looks! Good grief, my dear girl, your wedding is already lined up. Now we can't follow our heart and pursue this young man, can we? But who knows what kind of a man has been found for you! Could be an ugly old toad for all we know.'

'Oh, stop it.' Mali turned her face away.

'Are you upset because I'm telling the truth? Am I at fault for being able to read your mind? Why do you think the fellow has been so caring and concerned?'

'How should I know?'

'Shall I tell you? He did everything for the sake of that pretty face of yours. Beauty conquers all. It makes the upraised sword drop from the attacker's hand. Had the young man not fallen for you, would he have given two hoots for us? Anyway, I'm not complaining because I too have benefitted from his care and attention. As the saying goes, the string a garland is woven with gets as much adoration as the flowers.'

'Do you have a bad bout of indigestion, sister-in-law?'

'Do I? Oh, if I have, it may last for days on end. When the disease is in the mind, who cares what happens to the stomach?'

When the train stopped at Kharagpur, they asked the young man to send off a telegram to Govind to meet their train at Cuttack by nine in the evening.

Hema and Mali were tense again. Only a few hours remained before they were to get down. The young man had done so much for them, but they didn't know the first thing about him. He was so chivalrous, but they hadn't expressed a word of thanks. It would be wonderful if he too got down with them, because then they could get their people to make enquiries about him, find out where he was headed and how long he intended to stay in town.

In the end, throwing her hesitation and shyness out the window, Hema began to pelt the stranger with questions while expressing their gratitude for all his help and assistance.

But the young man was brief and guarded in his answers. He was from the west of the country, he was visiting his brother at Cuttack who worked there, he might look around for a job and stay on if he landed something suitable.

Hema and Mali decided to mention him to the family and see to it that they all helped him to land a good job. They might not be able to repay their debt, but it would be some consolation if they were instrumental in finding him employment at least.

Lachhamanji

'I don't know the lay of the land,' the young man said. 'I don't know where my brother is lodging. So what address can I give you? As for my name, well, it's Lachhmanji.'

As soon as the train steamed into Cuttack, the young man took off as if he was in an awful hurry. Govind had already arrived with a palanquin and was waiting anxiously and he heaved a sigh of relief when he found which compartment Hema and Mali were in. While Govind's son, Ram, helped unload the luggage, Hema confided in him. He should bring it to his father's attention that a Hindustani young man had helped them a lot during the tedious and difficult journey and that without his timely help and assistance the family could never have expected to find them safe and sound. Govind and his men then fanned out and tried their best to trace the young man, but he seemed to have vanished into thin air. Not satisfied with their efforts, Hema and Mali got their trusted old servant, Bhola, to search the platform one more time. To no avail, however. In the end, dejected and dispirited, the two women boarded the palanquin.

On the day of Mali's wedding, the whole village was in festive mood—music played, people chattered, waves of ululations rose; the din brought the sky down. Crying her heart out, Mali fell at the feet of her elders, saying goodbye and seeking their blessings. The plaintive notes of the shehnai rendered the atmosphere even more mournful. Many onlookers wept openly. Mali's mother was so numb from grief at the imminent prospect of parting from her beloved daughter that she slumped to the ground. Mali's father, a strong man of stern disposition, repeatedly wiped his bloodshot eyes and sat wrapped in silence, grunting only monosyllabic replies when pressed.

When all the wedding rituals were over, the customary games of fun and amusement began. The newlyweds were ushered into the inner quarters to indulge in a bit of gambling. A thick crowd of eager women and children thronged around them.

The moment Hema's eyes alighted on the bridegroom, she fell from the skies. 'Why, this is none other than our Lachhamanji!' she cried out, unable to hide her excitement. Mali stared from under her veil. The surprised onlookers began to look askance at one another.

When the bridegroom lowered his head with a sly smile, Hema didn't have the shadow of a doubt left. How could she have been wrong about someone she and Mali had spent a day and a half with on the train?

After she had recovered from the pleasant shock, Hema began to tease the groom mercilessly: 'Now, this doesn't pass for fair and proper gentlemanly conduct in our parts, no sir! First *he* puts on disguise to meet and chat up women from decent families and next he turns up kitted out as the bridegroom! It's a scam. I tell you this wedding is a scam. We'll never agree to giving away our darling girl to a Hindustani conman. How can anyone trust a fellow who changes his appearance like a chameleon? Did he have to come all the way from the western part of the country to become a lowly peon in our parts? But never mind, what's done is done. Now we will shower all our blessings on him and sincerely pray and hope that he remains an eternal slave of our dear Mali.'

The bridegroom gave a broad beaming smile. 'I'm yet to receive the summons from my mistress. If it's not forthcoming, I may have to try and seek employment elsewhere.'

Before the words were out of his mouth, someone landed a heavy blow on his back. 'Here's the summons. Take it.' The audience burst out laughing at the horseplay.

All rites, rituals and ceremonies done and over with, Hema accosted Mali. 'One just can't trust a modern girl of Kaliyug! I have suspected something was afoot since that day of the train journey. Tell me, how did you manage to communicate so much through your eyes, without even saying a word? You could have at least taken me into confidence. Were you afraid I would elope with your chosen one? Like Damayanti, you chose your Nala—although he was in disguise!'

When the story got around, Binod accosted Laxmidhar. 'Hey Lachhmanji, what about all that talk about the freedom of choice? Remember you poured scorn over the idea of arranged marriage? But in the end, you did meekly settle for marital servitude without a whimper! Of course, I know all about the power and pull of that sweet servitude. Male pride is swept aside like a blade of grass by the rushing stream of marital bliss, or like mighty elephants swept off by the Bhagirathi river. All our high-sounding philosophical discourses and scientific debates are of little avail, right?'

'Brother,' Laxmidhar smiled. 'Don't blame any of it on me. This must be in our stars. Who can dodge Providence?'

UPENDRA KISHORE DAS

The Flame: A Ghost Story

THE RAIN RESUMED, drumming hard on the wind-tossed fronds. The mud house, its thatch worn thin by seasons of rain and mist, stood forlornly in the middle of the wilderness, lost in the eerie darkness of the evening: its foundations were in ruins and from a couple of frail walls—ready to collapse at any moment—thorn bushes sprouted. The rain sputtered to a stop after a while. The clouds, streaking across the soot-black sky lit up as if by magic by lightning, rushed over the tender paddy seedlings, sending them into a tizzy.

From the dense foliage of a banyan tree standing behind the ruins, a fruit bat sailed out like a quivering cloud and headed for another tree, flapping its wings and sending down a spray of raindrops, before latching on to a branch and hanging from it upside down. A flame suddenly flickered in the cremation ground

---

'Daani Aalua' was first published in 1924 in *Baruni* Vol. I, No. 1.

The Flame: A Ghost Story

beyond the paddy fields and slowly moved until it was directly under the canopy of the big banyan, where it suddenly went out.

The bat started. 'Who's that?'

The flame flared up. 'Me.'

'Who're you? I don't know you.'

'You don't?' the flame gave a little laugh. 'You live in the banyan tree beside the house, don't you? But you don't know who used to live there!'

'I arrived here only four months ago.'

'Only four months ago? Oh, no wonder. When I'm talking of was a long time before that. Three or maybe four years ago I lived there with my husband; I didn't know what sorrow was. But the crash came quickly.' The flame paused, flickering pitifully.

A long moment passed.

'The whole thing now seems like a dream,' the flame continued. 'But even now my heart tightens and tears begin to choke me when I think back on it. I should try to forget it; why relive those bitter memories?'

The bat screeched and flapped its wings. 'Tell me about it,' it begged. 'Please. I want to hear about it.'

'You do, you really do? All right. Here we go:

Years have passed and now the house is in ruins, but when I arrived here as a new bride, it was awash with excitement and laughter. For some inexplicable reason, my husband decided to give up his studies in Cuttack and stay home; after our wedding he never went into town. I will never forget our first night together. Someone, perhaps a distant sister-in-law, pushed me into the bridal chamber and bolted the door from outside. A tiny brass oil lamp in a corner threw a pitiful light on the narrow bed in the middle of the room. Leaning heavily against the door, I found myself drenched in perspiration out of shame and shyness.

My husband was lying on the bed, his face to the wall. He started at the tinkling of my bangles. Getting up, he gently led me to the bed.

My hand within his was shivering like a palm frond. Moments passed. We were both tongue-tied. Then suddenly he pinched my hand—quite sharply, I remember; perhaps he was nervous—and burst out laughing: 'Oh, my shy little creeper! Only a year or two ago you used to frisk about before me like a little pony, remember? So don't pretend to be shy now, my darling.'

I laughed to myself. Every word he spoke was true. From childhood I had been besotted with him. How could I have known that I'd end up marrying him?

He led me to the bed and made me stretch out. Removing my veil, he held my face in both hands and whispered my name: 'Rati!'

I was too shy to answer.

'Won't you speak to me?'

I didn't answer.

'Have I become so distant in these last two years that you won't say a word? All right then, I'll leave.'

He got up off the bed.

'Don't.'

His face lighted up. He sat back down and drew me to him. 'Rati, do you remember that little incident one afternoon two years ago? Your sister-in-law wanted to play a joke on us and locked us in a room. It was then that I realized that it was not altogether impossible that you would become my wife. No one in your family was in favour of the match in the beginning, were they?'

The Flame: A Ghost Story

'My mother was,' I protested, my shame evaporating as he talked. 'She welcomed the match.'

'I knew as much, or else I'd have stopped going to your place after your father told me about your match with Brundavan.'

'Oh, come on, there were plenty of girls eager and willing to marry you,' I said.

He laughed. 'Maybe, but not the little one I yearned for. And who was that little one?'

A shiver of unbearable happiness tinged with shyness ran down my spine. Like a hungry madman, he put his arms around me and gushed: 'My good fortune, Rati, sheer good fortune. Thank God he granted the most important prayer of my life. I still can't believe that it's you who's beside me tonight.'

His lips touched mine. A moist gust of wind rushed in through the window and put out the lamp.'

The flame fell silent.

'Go on,' urged the bat.

The flame resumed:

'A year passed. But that first night remained the most extraordinary of my life. For the first time I realized how deeply he loved me. Ours was a small family—me, my husband and his grandmother. She was old and her vision very dim. Right from the first day, I had to put behind me the shyness of a new bride and get down to the household chores.

My husband wouldn't even consider going back to Cuttack, as if he couldn't bear the thought of being separated from me for a moment. We'd stick to our bedroom most of the time, looking at each other with lovesick eyes from morning to night, chattering away about this and that; day passed into night, but we didn't tire of each other's company.

Then one day—I remember it was raining just as hard as today—he went out somewhere. From the veranda I watched the rain and wind play hide and seek over the paddy fields stretching to the far horizon. He tiptoed stealthily up from behind and put his hands over my eyes. I gave a start. 'I know who it is,' I said.

'Who?'

'He.'

'Out with his name. You won't be released until then.'

I wanted to laugh out loud. 'But I don't know his name! Now away with you.'

He took his hands away and placed them on my shoulders. 'Rati!' His voice was pure honey.

'Mm!'

'You like the rain?'

'Very much.'

'Were you waiting for someone?' He gave a funny little smile.

I felt inexplicably mortified all of a sudden. 'Where have you been?' I asked, changing tack.

'To the old landlord's. His son Brundavan has returned home after a long time and I wanted to go and see him.'

'Brundavan? Which Brundavan?' Not the same one it had been all but settled I would marry!

He looked at me dubiously. 'You can't have forgotten him so soon! Only two years ago we used to come to your place together. And yes, some matchmaking went on between you two. Can you have forgotten all that?'

'Oh yes, now I remember.'

'He used to look me up every time he came to the village, but he

The Flame: A Ghost Story

stopped after we got married. One of these days I'll invite him over on your behalf.'

'Leave me out of it. If you want to invite him, go ahead and do it, but don't drag me into it.'

'All right,' he said, going off to change out of his wet clothes.

I fetched the vegetable basket from the store room and sat down to slice vegetables for dinner.

Then one day he brought Brundavan home.

It was evening and I was making the bed when I heard unfamiliar footsteps. I looked out and saw Brundavan at the door.

Seeing me, he drew back. I quickly pulled the end of my sari over my head and rushed out of the room. But I could hear him from the next room. I peeked from behind the door. How changed he looked! No longer as childlike as two years before, he was a grown man now, a perfect gentleman.

'Now that you're our landlord,' teased my husband, 'you might find it beneath your dignity to set foot in our house.'

'Stop pulling my leg, will you?' he protested. 'Half the blood in my veins has been formed from the heaps of rice puffs and rice flakes I've devoured here. You haven't forgotten that, have you?'

'But now you're the big landlord.'

'Stop talking nonsense or I'll never visit you again,' he said irritably.

My husband laughed. 'But my good friend, where have you been? You deigned to come only when I invited you.'

Brundavan lowered his head. 'Been awfully busy. But from now on, I mean to visit you regularly.'

I must have unconsciously wrung my hands in despair; the tinkling of bangles caught his attention and he said, 'I'd better be off. There's a lot of work to attend to. But I'll come again and very soon.'

My husband led the way holding a lantern and Brundavan followed him. For a moment he hung back to cast a lingering look in my direction before disappearing among the shadows.

My husband must have walked quite some distance to see him off, but I stayed on the veranda, leaning against a pillar until he returned.

'Did you see Brundavan?'

'Oh yes.' I feigned indifference.

'God's good man, isn't he?'

'I guess so.'

The next day Brundavan paid us a visit. My husband had him sit in the outer room and came inside. 'Where's grandma?' he enquired.

'In the next room saying her prayers. Why?'

'Brundavan wants to see her.' He went back to get his friend.

Brundavan met the old lady and when he came out of her room, he saw me on the veranda. 'Isn't that Rati?' he asked my husband.

'Of course.'

'My, she's become so shy! Until the other day she used to frisk about half-naked; now she's the big sister-in-law! She hasn't overcome her shyness,' and then he directed his next words at me, 'but my dear sister-in-law, I won't leave until I'm served puffed rice and scraped coconut from your own hands.'

I arranged some puffed rice and coconut on a plate and walked gingerly up to the door of the room where they were.

A strange shyness seemed to deaden my feet.

'How long will it take?' my husband shouted. 'Brundavan's getting impatient.'

I pulled the end of my sari over my head and tiptoed in.

'Have I become a stranger?' Brundavan laughed. 'Have you completely forgotten me?'

The Flame: A Ghost Story

I remained silent.

'I never suspected you'd be so shy with Brundavan,' my husband commented.

'Do you think of me sometimes?' Brundavan was insistent.

'Of course.' I was more or less forced to answer.

'But now when we meet you don't ask me a thing.'

'What would I ask?'

'Anything. Anything at all. How's my father, for example. And one more thing...'

I looked up at him in surprise.

'Tell me how to address you—by your name, or as sister-in-law?' and he burst out laughing.

'Oh God! That devil of a cat has sneaked back into the house again!' I mumbled, rushing out.

Brundavan's visits became too frequent and he made it his business to tease and joke with me. But somehow, I could never unwind in his presence and be as free with him as in the past. He didn't give up, however; he'd purposely frame his questions in such a manner that I was forced to answer, even though in monosyllables. Sometimes my husband, irritated, would say to his friend: 'Why waste your attention on someone who's so unresponsive?' I couldn't make out who he was irritated with—me or his friend. Now I know only too well, stupid little me; I should've caught on right then. Maybe if I'd realized in time, I would have saved myself from misfortune. But I guess my days of happiness were already counted and He who creates day and night had added up my account.

One morning, with the monsoon receding and the clouds gone, I was putting the damp and soggy mattresses and pillows out to dry. My husband called to me from our bedroom. 'Rati!'

I hurried inside. He was sitting on the bed.

'Come and sit by my side. I have something important to tell you.'

I went and sat beside him. He took my hand and nestled it in his lap. 'Rati, despite everything, we've managed to meet our needs until now. But what next?'

'Managed?' I was surprised.

'Despite our precarious finances, I haven't worked for nearly a year. Had I gone back to Cuttack, maybe I'd have landed a job long ago. How much longer can I sit idly by? Perhaps if we had enough land, I'd have been spared misfortune. How can we hang on unless I find some source of income immediately?'

'Does that mean you want to go off to Cuttack?' My voice quivered with trepidation.

'Is there any alternative?' he mumbled, hanging his head.

Fear gnawed at my heart. I clasped my hands around his neck and cried out piteously: 'No, no, please don't go to Cuttack. I'll die if you do.' I burrowed my face in his chest, drenching it with my tears.

He lifted my face with great tenderness and wiped away my tears. 'Did you imagine I'd go away and leave you on your own?' he laughed.

'Just a minute ago you said you would.' My doubt persisted.

'Just to scare you a little. Brundavan has promised me an accountant's job.'

My enthusiasm must have taken him by surprise. 'Oh yes, oh yes, that's infinitely better. He's making you a great offer. Take it. Don't ever go away to Cuttack or anywhere else, leaving me behind.'

'Brundavan is going to call this evening and I'm supposed to have my answer ready.'

My husband began the job the very next day. He left for the office after an early lunch and came home late in the evening and that was to become his routine. Some days he worked late into the night and my eyes would dry up watching for him to return.

One afternoon heavy clouds were hiding the sun and I was lolling in bed when I heard Brundavan's voice at the door. I sat up with a start. He walked up to me calmly, with a broad grin. 'Not able to sleep, huh, sister-in-law?'

'Oh no.'

What manner of a man was he that he plonked himself down beside me on the bed!

'Where's grandma?'

The way he was acting scared me. 'She's taking a nap.'

A moment passed.

'Rati!' he whispered.

'What?'

'Do you sometimes remember things from long ago? One day it was raining very hard and you asked me to make you paper boats to sail on the stream under your veranda and I asked you what you would give me in return. Do you remember your answer? You said you'd marry me. Somehow that playful reply of yours has stuck in my mind ever since.'

What's come over him? I wondered. Why's he talking like this? I sat as still as a wooden doll.

'Maybe that's why I haven't married,' he went on, 'turning down all the matches. So now you know who I've been waiting for. You also know who I find matchless, in looks as well as in qualities of the head and the heart, don't you, Rati?'

Outside, the rain began to pour. 'I've got the clothes to bring in,' I said, hurrying away and headed straight to where grandmother was sleeping, determined to keep away from Brundavan.

The old lady awoke hearing my footsteps. 'Who's that?'

I sat down beside her and without a word started massaging her feet.

That night, after dinner, as I stretched out beside my husband, I recounted the incident.

He was totally surprised. 'What time did he come?'

'In the afternoon. He knew you weren't here.'

His face clouded. 'Quite an untrustworthy fellow then, is our Brundavan,' he said. 'Better be on your guard.' The following day he changed his hours and stayed home in the afternoon. He began to go to the office towards evening. Naturally, he returned late at night. I began to breathe in relief, hoping that Brundavan would put an end to his unwelcome visits.

Perhaps Brundavan practised black magic. One afternoon, minutes after my husband had left, he arrived. I pretended not to see him, but he called out: 'Rati!'

'Yes, what is it?' I was forced to answer. 'Tell me. I've a lot of work to do, I can't wait.'

'Are you so busy that you won't even offer me a paan?'

I was irritated beyond belief, but what could I do? I rolled him some paans, wondering if he would sack my husband if I displeased him.

He stood by the window and when I held out the plate of paans, he grabbed my hands. 'Will you listen to me just this once?'

I shook my hands free with ill-concealed annoyance. 'What have you got to say?'

'Will you believe me? I . . . I always come here with the hope . . . the hope of one little word from your lips.'

My bones caught fire and I went mad with anger. But what could I do? I had to listen in silence.

'Not seeing you was a relief. But now, Rati, believe me, everything, including food, is like poison to me. The only thing I like to do is think about you. Will you always remain beyond my reach?' He inched closer and grabbed my hands again.

That made me seethe with anger. I pulled my hands out of his and rushed out of the room. 'If you're truly a gentleman,' I said, 'never step inside this house again.'

'All right.' He left quietly, crestfallen.

I pretended not to have heard him.

As usual, my husband came home late in the evening and the first thing he asked at dinner was: 'Did Brundavan come by today?'

'Yes.' I was dying to unburden myself, but a strange sense of shame prevented me.

He didn't pursue the matter further; he finished dinner, washed his hands and went to bed. He was so grim and quiet that my courage failed me to bother him with questions.

Two days later I learnt that he'd given up his job.'

The flame fell silent again, growing dimmer as if about to go out.

The bat began to screech: 'Don't leave the story unfinished. Tell me the rest.'

Very softly, almost inaudibly, the flame continued:

There isn't much to tell. It's too agonizing; it breaks my heart to think about it; even now it burns fresh holes into my disembodied heart.

When my husband gave up his job, I was secretly relieved, happy even; I was safe from Brundavan's torments.

But from then on, my husband seemed to have changed; he no longer exulted in my company as before. Not only did he stop speaking nicely to me, he began to avoid me like the plague. Only if he absolutely had to, would he bark a word or two, making a long face. I knew in my bones the happy days were over.

Sometimes I so wanted to ask what was eating him up, but merely seeing his sombre face would petrify me; I knew he was just waiting to fly off the handle. I'd cry silently deep into the night, until long after he was asleep. Sometimes I toyed with the idea of putting an end to my miserable life. Slipping down the steps into the bottomless depths of the pond would not have been too difficult. Sometimes I would walk to the pond at midday, but a precious little life was already kicking inside me. How could I simply up and die! Slowly I would retrace my steps home.

But now I feel I should have jumped into the water. That would have put a quick end to my misery. But my fate was far worse and could not be avoided so easily.

Another day, a day of pouring rain just like today, as if it were the end of the world—the cold wind and rain making the mighty trees chatter—my husband walked off, taking offence on some slight pretext. The whole day passed and evening came, but he was nowhere in sight; my eyes had already become dry, watching the path. Regret gnawed at my heart; I started berating myself: Why did I have to answer him back? Why couldn't I restrain myself? When would he return? What was he up to?

Then I heard a voice outside. My heart jumped. Had he come back at last? I rushed out. But it was only Brundavan.

He seemed to be in great agitation. 'Rati,' he said, his voice laden with anxiety. 'Fetch a lantern and come with me. Your husband's been bitten by God knows what. He's lying in the backyard. Make haste. Quick.'

My head began to swim and everything around me went black. I didn't have a moment to think. Grabbing a lantern, I rushed out after him.

The Flame: A Ghost Story

I was worried sick. What had bitten my husband? Not a snake, please oh God! The very thought of it was killing me, my power to think clearly fast seeping away. I hardly realized how far from home I had already walked. Suddenly I stopped. Where was I heading? Where was Brundavan leading me? We had left our backyard way behind and were now at the edge of the village. I refused to take another step forward. 'Brundavan,' I called out.

Where was he? There was nobody around; I was all alone in the middle of nowhere. Fear gripped my heart and my blood turned to water.

The rains stopped, the clouds parted and like whitewash the moonlight glistened on the mossy dark earth. I gathered my wits about me and broke into a breathless run towards home. I stopped only once I had reached the door, my heart thudding violently.

Inside, there was a lamp burning and in the middle of the room stood my husband staring at the doorway.

The whole thing had been a hoax, a vile little trick of Brundavan's; but it had dawned on me far too late.

My husband came charging out. 'Where have you been?' He clenched his teeth in wild anger. 'Tell me the truth.'

My head was going round and round; I was unable to utter a word. 'You don't have to tell me. I know. I know everything. I don't need to hear a word. Now beat it, get the hell out of my sight.' He gave me a mighty push.

I lost my balance and toppled over face forward. All I'll ever remember was that when my heavy belly hit the threshold my heart burst and blood spurted out of my mouth like a stream. I never regained consciousness. I delivered a stillborn baby while in a coma and died shortly afterwards, the last flicker of life sputtering out.

Next morning, a contrite Brundavan made a clean breast of it. My poor husband went crazy from guilt and grief. He burst out sobbing like a child and clutching my lifeless hand, wailed: 'Rati, my darling, forgive me. Forgive me just this once. I've behaved abominably, like a fool, a beast ...' His anguish was so deep I wanted to return to life again, but that was not within my power.

He hugged me and cried, 'Rati, come back. Come back, dear Rati. Never again will I become angry with you.'

He went raving mad and vanished from home.

People carried my body to the cremation ground beyond the paddy fields. They buried my stillborn child somewhere there. My pyre was lit and the all-consuming flames reduced my body to ashes in no time. I was left with only this flickering light, which is as real to me as a veranda.

The flame fell silent.

'Is that why you wander about in the dark?' the bat asked. 'Always looking for your child?'

There was no answer; only the wind hissed through the tree like a sharp, indrawn breath: Shhh ... shhh ... shhh ...

SUPRABHA KAR

The Long Wait

She was a fallen woman. Usually, a fallen woman is looked down upon by the whole world, but anyone who saw her beautiful face, her deep, dark, starry eyes full of remorse and anguish, was profoundly moved and lost his contempt.

She rose before the birds started calling at dawn, walked to the Manikarnika ghat of Kasi to take a dip in the holy Ganga, the morning star her only witness. She'd then hurry to Lord Bisweshwar's temple, where she'd offer flowers to the deity and, silently, pour forth her grief.

The old temple priest couldn't help being impressed by the woman's devotion and, when, at the end of the service, her streaming tears fell at the Lord's feet, the old man's eyes watered too. Once, he even felt as if the stone pedestal of the deity was shaking at the sight of the poor grief-stricken woman.

'Pratiksha' was first published in 1925 in *Utkal Sahitya*, Vol. 29, No. 5

The old man was so moved that one day he placed his hands on her head and gently asked, 'Daughter, who are you? Why do you come here day after day and shed tears? Your devotion is so intense that it even makes the Lord's stone pedestal shake. Look at me, I've been here for ages and have cried before Him for who knows how long, but never have I witnessed the slightest tremor in His countenance. Tell me, who are you?'

She shrank from the old priest's kindness. 'Does God really listen to my prayers and entreaties? If He did, why do I remain enveloped in my grief?'

'God listens to everyone's prayers, daughter.'

'That's the belief that brings me to this temple every day to shed tears, so He might absolve me of all my sins and give me shelter in His bosom.'

'What causes your grief, child? What sins have you committed?'

The causes of her grief, the sins she'd committed? Could she divulge them? Who'd make sense of her grief, fathom its depths? She remained silent.

But when the old priest insisted, Malati raised her head and looked into his eyes. 'You can't imagine, you won't understand, no, you can't. No one can plumb the depths of my depravity and despair. There's no end to the sins I've committed. I'm so low I'm not fit to enter this temple.'

Flummoxed, the old priest stared at her. 'Who are you?'

'A fallen woman,' Malati replied, slow and unhurried. 'A whore.'

The old man started. It was worse than being struck by a thunderbolt. 'Sinner!' he shrieked. 'How dare you defile this sacred space? Go away, leave. This instant!'

The Long Wait

Not wishing to further offend, Malati stepped out obediently, but so heart-wrenching was her contrition that it pierced the old priest's heart and revived a long-forgotten memory. Trembling and in tears, he enquired, 'Why did you get into that, mother?'

His kindness only made Malati burst into another flood of tears. 'Why did I get into that?' she asked, her voice breaking. 'That's what I keep asking myself—why did I get into it?'

After a long pause, she began: 'I never received any love and affection right from birth. After four daughters, I was utterly unwelcome: my mother dissolved in tears and my father turned his face away. As I grew older, I burnt with shame whenever I compared myself to my elder sisters. I was so dark. I began to understand the reason behind my father's long, long sighs.

'When I reached a marriageable age, the suitors came. It took a while to gather why they came forward to marry a dark-complexioned girl like me. My father had promised a dowry of four thousand rupees. That was a lot of money by any reckoning, not an easy sum to put by. No wonder, many a young man showed his eagerness to marry me.

'One day, one such suitor turned up at our door in the dead of the night, with drums and fireworks and tied the wedding knot. The next day I left my parents' place forever and went to live with the stranger's family. On that one occasion, my poor mother, in helpless tears, pressed me to her bosom. Perhaps she knew what was in store for me.

'My days in that new place passed not too unpleasantly at first. But as the memory of the four thousand rupees slowly receded, the love and affection of my husband dried up, until there was nothing left. On top of everything, he began to drink heavily and became an alcoholic. My mother-in-law never forgave me for it: I was the one to blame, I was an evil curse, I'd driven her son to it ever since I set foot in their home.

'As days, months and years passed, I was subjected to unrelenting torture. All of it inflicted by my kind husband. My mother-in-law didn't hesitate to stoke the fires of his anger. Many were the days and nights I'd simply pass out from the savage beatings; never once did anyone in the entire household utter a word of sympathy.

'Still, I overcame my grief as long as I could see the face of my son—the apple of my eye. But he too deceived me. He died an untimely death. How could I have not suffered every bit of misfortune etched on my forehead? My poor boy came down with a fever and died in three days without a drop of medicine. "Ma," he called out to me feebly at the last moment, stretching his tiny, fevered hands. "Ma." I could take it no more, I'd had enough. I decided to consign my grief and pain to the cold bosom of the river that ran past the village. I was on the verge of drowning myself when I let someone dissuade me. He lured me with the promise of a job and shelter. I fell for it. I was willing to become a maidservant in someone's place to escape my husband's beatings. Besides, I could not stomach going back to the home where there wasn't anyone to call me "Ma." So, with one last tearful glance at the house I had lived in until then, I eloped with my rescuer.

'After the novelty and excitement had worn off, I realized I'd lost everything. The world had shut all its doors on me. Not a shred of consideration for my suffering from any quarter, no evaluation of my "sin". It forced me down the only path, the only option, left open to me. My heart quailed at the very thought of it and I was filled with self-loathing and disgust, but who else could carry my burden for me? Society gave me an epithet too—whore!

'The man who had taken advantage of a grieving mother's weakness to drag her down the sinful slope is still being lauded and looked upon as respectable. Do you have any idea what bitterness flooded my being against this injustice? I wanted to wage a rebellion against God. I wanted to unmask all who had reduced me to my pitiable plight, even if it meant eternal hell and damnation for me. I wanted to force open people's eyes to their mistaken values and notions. You can't simply cast an innocent woman into the cauldron of contempt without considering the circumstances of her degradation.

'But I couldn't go on. What stopped me from continuing on the sinful path was the throbbing memory of my little son. I'd often hear the voice of that innocent one and half year old: "Ma." How would I experience the love of that pure and innocent flower if I didn't rid myself of my own sinful ways? I was so full of anguish that the dam burst and my sorrow gushed forth in an uncontrollable flood of tears. In the midst of my darkest despair, I was able to make out a beacon of light. I came away to this city, but there's not a sliver of safety and shelter for me here either. Just to evade the prying eyes of the curious, to ward off their hundred and one questions, I took to rising before cockcrow, to offer my prayers at the Lord's lotus feet while it was still quite dark. I've laid bare my soul before Him—all the faults and weaknesses of my character which betrayed and brought me to this sorry fate. Has God no pity for me, does my sin weigh so heavily that even His doors are shut to me?'

The old priest, his eyes brimming with tears, was speechless for a long time. Then extending his feeble and trembling hands, he pulled Malati to his bosom and kissed her on the forehead.

After so long, she seemed to have found a little nook of love and sympathy in somebody's heart.

Malati's devotion to the old man, her loving care of him, the peals of her sweet laughter not only strengthened the bonds of the old priest's attachment, it stoked his fears too. People were getting nosey, tongues were wagging. Who was the young woman whose laughter enlivened the old priest's humble abode? Who was she who hung at the door with the old man's two-year-old grandson to welcome him with a sweet smile and wipe away all traces of his tiredness at the end of a long day?

How long could they be put off?

When confronted directly, the old man stuck to his line: 'She's my long-lost daughter who has come back.'

His grandson had taken to Malati too. Twining his delicate little arms around her neck, he took to addressing her as 'Ma'. Ma! That would make her nostalgic: pressing the boy to her bosom, she would relive the memory of her dead child.

But the fear that nagged the old priest's mind came true one day. Malati's past was out in the open.

There was a huge uproar. If the old man didn't drive the woman out of his home, he'd be removed from his position of the temple priest. A new priest would be engaged, a fake priest like him could not be allowed to carry on the holy services. He'd be branded as an immoral man too, for sheltering a whore.

The sky seemed to fall on Malati's head. Why should a man at such a ripe old age have to suffer such ignominy? Just because he had offered her shelter? 'Throw me out,' she begged him. 'Let me go far away from here. I can put up with any amount of humiliation myself, but not what is being reserved for you.' She dissolved in a torrent of tears and every drop that fell from her eyes struck the old man's heart like a stone.

But his love for her only deepened. 'Hmm.' That was his only response to all her pleadings.

'Ma,' the child said, tugging at the end of her sari. 'Ma.'

Finally, the old priest confronted the crowd. 'Listen brothers, I can't accept your wishes and drive my daughter out of my home.'

'Then you must leave the temple.'

'Fair enough,' the old priest said with a sigh, his eyes riveted on the deity. 'If it pleases you, so be it. I'll leave the temple today, but I'll never give up on my daughter.'

He stood in front of the deity for a long time before leaving the temple for good. In the gathering darkness of the evening, he turned his head one more time for one last glimpse of the Lord. Tired, his dim eyes swimming in tears, he cloaked his deep sense of hurt behind a benign smile and hurried down the steps.

His humble abode stood as before: the evening lamp burnt brightly as in the past, but the eyes and face of the person who waited by the door to welcome him and who was the source of his joy and delight, was missing. He sat down on the veranda and called out: 'Where're you, mother?'

No answer. He called again. But still no one came running out.

Full of fear and anxiety, the old man stepped inside. The child was fast asleep on a mattress, a lighted lamp burnt brightly by his bedside. Noticing the piece of paper tucked under the lamp, he picked it up and read it. It was a message written by Malati.

'I'm leaving this world. I'm a vile curse. Not only did I ruin my life, I brought grief to the one who sheltered me. May your kind fatherly heart bless me that I find peace on the other side of life.'

Picking up the sleeping child and clutching him to his breast, the old man ran in the direction of the river. Searching as far as he could with his dimming vision, he noticed a spot where the river was at its deepest. Something seemed to bob up and down a few times before sinking without a trace.

From then on, the old man would go every evening with the child and wait patiently on the riverbank, full of hope. Who knows, his anxious waiting might bring the dead back from the valley of death. The child would often ask: 'Where is Ma?' The old man would press him to his breast and point vaguely to a spot where sky and water seemed to merge.

BISWANATH RATH

The Witch

A WINTER EVENING IN the month of Pausa. The untouchables' colony of Badoi village with its low, thatched huts was coming alive. Deserted during the day—not even a fly around to swat—the place was beginning to vibrate and throb with life. The hustle and bustle of people going about their chores, calling out greetings to one another, picking or patching up quarrels, playing the khanjani and lifting their voices in songs and prayers. The place was never more awake.

The music medley met that evening as it regularly had since the advent of winter. Some racy, spicy Baishnav Pani numbers were belted out. But the classical chhanda numbers—especially 'The Past is Long Gone, Sweetheart,' without which no music session could ever be concluded— were missing. The chhanda specialist Padia was nowhere in sight.

'Daani' was first published in 1935 in *Nav Bharat*, Vol. 2, No. 4.

'He's unlikely to put in an appearance tonight,' a musician said, tired of hitting the khanjani. 'Sahu the moneylender has summoned him. And Pitei too. Apparently, Pitei has possessed the moneylender's young daughter and sucked her blood. I tell you, that awful woman has become such a die-hard witch that she can suck blood off anyone in broad daylight!'

'Oh, really?' The man playing the cymbals stopped. 'I had no idea she's so far gone already! Now that you mention it, I do recollect having seen her getting up to her tricks in the cremation ground. It must be she who possessed my son the other day. Wonder why Padia continues to give her shelter. If I were in his place, I'd have unceremoniously driven her out long back. Anyway, that's none of my business. Let Padia face the music. And now I better hurry and get Mani Jena to chant a charm on my child to ward off the evil eye.'

'Listen to this, folks,' said the man whose part it was to repeat the last line after the lead singer. 'This is something I saw with my own two eyes. It was early in the day, just about mid-morning, or perhaps maybe the bathing hour, when the newborn calf of Brother Bhobana—that was frisking about merrily—suddenly dropped dead. Seems Pitei had clapped her eyes on the poor thing as she was passing by. She was returning from the paddy fields carrying a bundle of corn balanced on her head. In less than half an hour, a perfectly hale and hearty calf was gone. I tell you, Sahu's daughter must have been out all by herself and run full tilt into Pitei. The sight of a tender young thing like her must have made the witch go berserk.'

That evening, in Padia's absence, the music session proved a

The Witch

damp squib, but the bone-chilling stories about witches that went round more than made up for it.

Pitei, Padia's elder brother's widow, was dark, pockmarked, with protruding front teeth; her face was triangular, chin pointed and her eyes were sunken. She looked every inch a witch. People spoke of her as 'the witch' behind her back, but not to her face. They all feared her, even the hardened harridans, for they all had young children in the family and every kid was a sitting duck for a witch.

When Pitei became a childless widow at a very young age, a couple of remarriage proposals had come her way. A one-eyed man and a hump-backed one, with little hopes of landing a good-looking bride, were willing to marry her, but both backed out at the last minute when they heard the village talk about her. So Pitei remained in Padia's house as she had nowhere to go. Sometimes when she wore the one yellow sari she possessed—kept carefully folded and mothballed in her wicker basket—the villagers would titter: 'Make no mistake, this time Pitei's going to get married for sure.'

Pitei returned home with Padia late at night. Sahu's servant had struck her again and again with his brass-tipped stick, until people had lost count. No one told her the reason, but she could gather from what she overheard that she was paying the price of possessing the moneylender's daughter and sucking her blood. She had heard many a tale about witches herself, so it wasn't difficult for her to put two and two together. Instead of streaming, the tears simply dried up in her eyes. Was she really a witch? She could scarcely believe it. Perhaps that's why she was able to endure that sound thrashing. She remembered how in the past the village children often placed a braided straw rope across her path. As she nimbly skipped over it, she'd wonder who the witch was; for whom the rope was meant. She remembered how on earlier occasions, the village women shielded their newborns from her on one pretext or the other. She had never understood why.

Had it been some other time, Pitei wouldn't have taken the beating lying down; she'd have hit back. But tonight, she was so shell-shocked that she couldn't even give out a squeak, let alone cry. Did everyone in the village really believe she was a blood-sucking witch?

Already the news had spread through the village. Pitei had become a full-blown witch. How could anyone who was not a full sixteen-anna witch be able to endure that savage beating? A lesser witch would have dropped to the ground.

As she followed Padia to his place, Pitei ran several snippets of her life through her mind again and again. Was she really a witch? When had she become one? Why, Padia had never treated her as one! She had always picked up his little son and petted and fondled him, fussed and fawned on him; the little one seemed to enjoy her company too. Padia, God bless him, had never cast aspersions on her or made her feel small. When, after the death of her husband, she had nowhere to go, Padia had asked her to stay on. Even when the whole village turned against her and castigated her, Padia hadn't spoken a word against her. If he had believed the villagers, would he have given her shelter? Would he have let her pick up and hold his newborn son?

When she reached Padia's house, she found a straw rope placed in front of the threshold from end to end. Padia's wife was sitting by the hearth with her child on her lap. Pitei's heart sank. Did

The Witch

Padia's wife too believe the canard? Maybe the straw rope hadn't been placed before the front door on purpose? What if it had fallen there somehow. But it was laid out so neatly!

As soon she stepped inside, Padia's wife Champa started and hurried to cover her child with the end of her sari. Already her eyes had popped out when she saw Pitei nimbly step across the straw rope. She looked at Padia meaningfully: Have you ever seen a witch as brazen as this? Even the rope of straw hadn't stopped her.

Pitei slumped in her corner of the room. Images sailed past her vision—the road, the river, her husband, Padia's little son. The images began to melt and merge in a jumble and eventually took the shape of a hazy road—the Jagannath Sadak. Would she now have to hit that road? Was that her destiny, her future?

In the muddle of her thoughts, she didn't know when her eyes had closed and she had nodded off. But her sleep didn't last long—it never does when one is as ravenously hungry as she was. She looked around. Champa was alone by the hearth; Padia and the little one were nowhere in sight. Outside, it was raining hard and ropes of water dripped from the holes in the thatch. The hut was being buffeted by gusts of violent wind. She thought maybe more than hunger, it was the bone-chilling cold that had awakened her.

Padia returned home with his son in the small hours, both soaked to the skin. The little child was already shivering and shaking. Pitei raised her head to get a better look. Tied around the child's neck were a couple of palm leaves strung together with a thread; an amulet was fastened to his arm. The shocking realization dawned on her that she was being held responsible for all the tortures the poor little child had been subjected to. That made her break into silent sobs. How she longed to take the child on her lap, dry him, massage his limbs and pet him.

'Did the exorcist do a thorough job?' Champa asked Padia in a hoarse whisper. It was meant to be inaudible, but Pitei heard every word.

'Hush!' Padia replied, his voice low. '*She* might become enraged if she gets the hang of it. But don't you worry, I'll throw her out of our home in a couple of days.'

Pitei heard that too.

Before the night was over, the little one came down with a raging fever. When he began to bawl, Champa woke up. Pitei was missing. Her son's little body was burning up. She jolted Padia awake and asked him to hurry to the exorcist.

She sat beside the unconscious child. Instead of coming down, the fever was fast shooting up. The child began to wheeze and choke, his mouth shut and nose clogged. Suddenly he started convulsing, then stiffened and grew cold to the touch. Champa panicked. Padia hadn't returned.

All of Champa's tears were in vain. Long before Padia could return with the exorcist, the boy was dead. When Padia reached home, all he could hear was his wife's heart-rending howling: 'Oh my treasure, oh my precious!'

The news of the child's death and Pitei's disappearance spread through the village in no time. A few village elders came forward to console Padia: 'What do you expect when you keep a snake at home? It'll bite you some day. What good does it do now to cry? The wicked witch sucked the life out of the little one because she was angry with you.'

The Witch

Champa continued to wail bitterly, hitting her head on the ground again and again. 'Oh my treasure, oh my precious! Why did I give shelter to a witch who sucked out your life!'

Away from the village, far from everyone and well along on the Jagannath Sadak, Pitei dabbed her moist eyes with her sari-end and tried to wipe the unfair stigma pinned on her by a cruel, heartless world.

BHAGABATI CHARAN PANIGRAHI

The Kill

Ghinua was known to be the greatest marksman around, using a bow and arrows he himself had fashioned. To shoot, he would lie on his back, nock his arrow, pull it back right to his ear and send it piercing home. He could hit a target a mile away. He had killed countless deer, sambar, wild boars, bears, leopards, but only two tigers. For shooting the tigers, he had received rewards.

One morning, Ghinua climbed the stairs to the deputy commissioner's bungalow with a sack. His bow hung from one shoulder, his axe rested on the other and in his hand, he held the quiver full of arrows.

The orderly was shocked to see him in such a state. 'Hey, what've you brought today?' He knew Ghinua quite well. He had often taken a cut from Ghinua's rewards.

'Shikar' was first published in 1936 in *Adhunika*, Vol. 1, No. 1.

The Kill

Ghinua did not answer. He merely displayed two rows of dirty, yellowing teeth. There was no knowing whether it was a smile or a grimace. Nobody had ever seen Ghinua laugh. On rare occasions, he just bared his teeth, as he was doing now.

'Hey, why won't you say what've you brought today? What kill?'

Ghinua pointed to the sack. 'A deadly beast.'

'A tiger?'

Ghinua shook his head.

'A leopard?'

Ghinua shook his head again.

'A bear? A boar?'

Ghinua merely shook his head.

'What on earth then?'

The sound of their voices drew the sahib out of his room. Ghinua promptly prostrated himself before the white man and bared his teeth. When the sahib expressed his desire to see the kill, he opened the sack, took out a human head and placed it ceremoniously at the sahib's feet.

The sahib jumped back.

'Baksheesh, sahib!' Ghinua stretched out his hand.

With the greatest effort, the sahib curbed his fear and indicated with a nod for Ghinua to wait. He went inside and telephoned the police station for an armed contingent. He knew armed policemen would be needed to overpower Ghinua: the man had the strength of a monster and was armed with his lethal bow and arrows.

When Ghinua was led away in police custody, his hands and feet manacled, he could not understand. 'Why did they put me in chains?' he asked, whenever he had a chance. Some said that he would be hanged, others that he would be deported beyond the black waters to jail in the Andamans. But why? What crime had he committed? He did not understand what people said.

One day when the deputy commissioner came to inspect the jail, Ghinua asked him what all the fuss was about. The deputy commissioner explained to him that for killing a tiger, he had been given his reward promptly. This time, though, he had killed a human being and the amount of reward would have to be determined by six or seven wise men; therefore, it would take some time. After all, one didn't kill human beings too often. Ghinua found the explanation quite satisfactory.

When the trial began, Ghinua thought perhaps he was to be given his baksheesh now. With much gusto, he gave the details of the killing to the judge. It hadn't been at all easy to kill a man like Govind Sardar. There were quite a few hunters on his trail, but no one had succeeded; Govind Sardar had always eluded them because he travelled in a motor car. The man had accumulated great wealth by cheating others out of their property. A diabolical man, he had murdered countless people, molested many helpless women and reduced numerous others to penury. Not only had he snatched away Ghinua's property, but on that fateful evening he had been on the verge of molesting Ghinua's wife. What audacity the man had! When he saw Ghinua, he quickly hopped into his motor car and tried to drive away. But it wasn't easy to escape Ghinua. He shot an arrow and deflated a tyre and when the car came to a stop, without any ado he chopped off Govind Sardar's head. Out of breath, he ran all the way to the deputy commissioner's bungalow. Govind Sardar was no mean opponent when it came to a fight. He always carried a gun and people were more afraid of him than of tigers and bears. He was more dangerous than the wild animals.

The Kill

And Ghinua had shown great courage and skill to hunt down such a fellow. Some years ago, the sahib had given a baksheesh of five hundred rupees to Dora for killing Jhapat Singh, the rebel leader. But Jhapat Singh was a saint compared to Govind Sardar. Jhapat Singh had never raped a woman, nor taken anyone's property by force; he had merely looted the government treasury and bumped off a few sepoys. Govind Sardar was a far more despicable person. Ghinua ought to get a baksheesh bigger than Dora's for killing him.

Everyone in the courtroom burst out laughing at his story.

'Yes, you'll be given a fat baksheesh,' chortled the judge.

'Indeed, you've been brought here to be given the baksheesh!' the government prosecutor added.

Ghinua did not catch on to their jokes and jibes. He always took everything seriously. He never understood such things.

The sentence was passed. Ghinua could not follow even one word of it. Later, when he was led away to the jail, he enquired about it and was told that the day of the baksheesh was not far off.

Not for a moment did it occur to Ghinua that he was a criminal and that he had been condemned to death. How was he to know that killing Jhapat Singh was not the same as killing Govind Sardar? It did not register in his mind that while the first was considered as an act of bravery, the second was an offence. He simply didn't have the head to delve into the subtleties of the white man's laws. After all, wasn't he just a savage?

If Dora could be given five hundred rupees for killing Jhapat Singh, Ghinua continued to think in his cell, why should he be given a lesser reward? No, he wouldn't accept it; he would throw down the money and tell the sahib point blank: 'Better not give me anything, sahib. But surely, I deserve more than what you gave Dora.'

In the dark lonely cell, he thought of this and many other things. He did not have a soul to turn to, nor had he any desire to talk. He was growing restless. All he wanted was to collect his reward and get back home to his wife.

Then came the day of the execution. He was asked what his last wish was.

'My baksheesh!' he said.

'All right, come along now. You'll get your baksheesh.'

As he was led away, a black hood slipped over his head, he thought: The government certainly has many fancy rules and regulations before bestowing a big reward. Look at the fuss. But then, after all, it's a big occasion and how can it be done without a little ceremony! When I get back home, I'll show the baksheesh around. How happy my wife will be! I'll build us a new house, buy farmland to cultivate and settle down quietly. No Govind Sardar will be around to rob me again. Maybe, I'll ...

He never knew what hit him.

GOPINATH MOHANTY

Dã

Before the crack of dawn, the old woman Dã, short for Domi, awoke with a start to the rhythmic pounding of husking paddles coming from the direction of the fishermen's quarters in the village. Through the cracks and crevices of her mud-plastered hut, she could see the light dawning.

She ran her eyes around her tiny room.

Not a soul around. No one—totally empty.

Not so two score years ago, when she'd first set foot here; but of course, back then she didn't have to lie in or rise from bed alone. Her hair hadn't yet turned grey, nor was her bosom flaccid and covered with wrinkles, nor her eyes so sunken in their sockets that you could pour a fistful of grain into them.

Outside the door, the dog Banka thumped its tail.

'Oh God, not so early in the day!' Domi shouted. 'Miserable mutt, don't you get started so early. Beat it. Out. Out.'

'Dã' was first published in 1936 in *Adhunika*, Vol. 1, No. 2.

Old crone Domi, Bhaji Behera's youngest daughter, had once been young, lascivious and desirable. In the full bloom of youth, she'd go alone into the mango groves to sweep up and collect dry leaves and twigs. She had only herself to blame for wantonly drifting along and finally landing in that wasteland of what was now her home, right in Sada Mohanty's bed. What a journey that had been! How many years had passed since? She remembered it like yesterday.

A stout stick in hand, Gada Mohanty was up before dawn to keep watch on his son Sada, who had gone astray and taken to spending nights out. What father would let his boy go to the dogs just because his poor mother had died?

But even as Gada set up watch at the front door, the boy made good his escape through the back. And the hussy that Domi was, would smile sarcastically at the old man and call out, 'Good morning, master!' More a taunt than a polite greeting. What a war of words that would unleash. Domi had strength in her vocal cords then, however, and was brazenly dissolute besides. In the end, it was Gada who had to beat a retreat, accused of surreptitiously digging up yams from Bholi Behera's backyard, an unbearable humiliation.

Despite all that fracas, Domi had managed to settle on a bit of Gada Mohanty's land—the patch Sada Mohanty had inherited— as Sada's mistress, his all-purpose-maid.

Ah! The memories of her romance made her rheumy eyes twinkle in their craters. Her two large yellowing teeth sank mirthfully into her thick, chapped lips in a smile, as a last hurrah over the shadows of death.

'Not so early, you blasted mutt,' she shouted at the dog on the other side of the door. 'Beat it. Someone, drive it away.'

Dā

Tail tucked between his hind legs, his pointy ears twitching, Banka slunk away from the old woman's door, leaving behind his mongrel stink, strands of wet fur, ticks, flies and mosquitoes from his coat.

Domi began her day carrying the dead weight of sixty years. Piles and piles of chores awaited her, myriads of them—from sweeping and swabbing the floor and walls with cow-dung paste, to washing soiled nappies, to scouring the pots and pans. A familiar enough routine, but today she didn't feel up to it, her otherwise insensible heart in a turmoil.

The villagers often remarked it was for this ability to work hard that Sada had seduced her and made her give up her parental home, her caste and throw in her lot with him. But if what people said was true, her whole life was nothing but a shambles. Even after all these years, she couldn't believe what they were saying.

There was the patch of greens on which she had once slept with Sada. She tended it with love, sprinkled water on it every day and diligently removed the weeds and grass.

While doing the dishes at the well, she fell to looking back over her life. There had been more sorrow than happiness; more curses, abuses and harsh words than kind and sweet ones; more slogging and slaving for others than seeing to her own comfort and leisure. She had never had a good meal or nice clothes. The few days of happiness and bliss she had enjoyed lay buried under the relentless years of deprivation, which had turned her hair grey, compromised her health, dimmed her eyes and sunk them into their sockets.

'Away with you, damn dog,' she shouted, catching sight of Banka. 'Get a stick someone. Beat the cur. The lousy dog has turned up here too, just for a pitiful handful of rice, which has become dry and hard as stone.'

Suddenly she remembered one of those days from the ancient past.

'*Hey Domi, why are you all smiles today?*'

'*Hey Domi, whoever gave you that silly name—Domi? You ought to have been named Pemi instead.*'

'*Hey girl, hold on. Don't rob me of every little paisa. Do you see this bundle I've got for you? Guess what's in it.*'

The old woman's eyes dreamily wandered off to the three-branched date palm bending beneath the ghost-eaten coconut palm in the backyard, the utensils slipping out of her hands.

'Hey Dā, you old witch, are you done with the utensils yet?'

It would take some shouting and scolding from Malli's mother, Sada Mohanty's widow, to stem the flow of her tender memories. She hurried up with her chores.

As she carried the pots and pans inside, Sana's mother opened the door, her face swollen as much from long hours of sleep as from the wad of paan tucked into her mouth the night before. 'What rotten luck,' the woman grumbled out loud when she saw Domi. 'Whose face to look upon first thing in the morning!'

That was the cue for a lively mud-slinging match.

When it was over, Sana's mother left for her bath.

Domi had to hurry—get fuelwood, collect some greens, rustle up something for the kids or else the brood would go hungry. She had to take care of all that. Who else would? She was part of the family.

As soon as Sana's mother headed for her bath, Domi, casting glances at the pond, threw open the wicker gate of her patch of greens and raised her voice for all to hear, 'Woe is me, those damn cows again! The moment their mistress turns her back the damn animals get into her patch! Run, you beasts!. Go away, wretches.'

She stacked dry bamboo sticks against Malli's mother's house and then slipped into Sana's mother's patch to reach for a pumpkin growing on a vine.

Morning turned to midday.

After everyone had eaten and gone off for a siesta, Domi sat down to her meal: just a bowl of watered rice. 'Hey, daughter-in-law,' she shouted. 'It's just water, no rice. Death should take me. They gorge on all sorts of delicacies but leave not a morsel of anything for me! Do they ever touch watered rice? No wonder they've eaten this family out of home and hearth.'

The children picked up the refrain: 'Gorge on, gorge on!'

'Wait until I slap the life out of you!' Domi retaliated.

'What did you say? You dare say that?'

Then there was a no-holds-barred quarrel. Domi spewed venom with every mouthful and ended her tirade after she had stuffed herself with watered rice.

An afternoon of silence.

Time for Dā to start washing the dirty dishes.

As she set about it, she stopped short. Her eyes fell on a boy hidden in the lantana bushes laden with clusters of tiny ripe fruit. Who was he—Sautia? Couldn't be anyone else! He alone wore that rag of a striped towel. But who was the girl with him—Malli? She had her face buried in the crook of the boy's neck. And the ravenous look on the boy's face—not much different from what she, Domi, had seen on Sada's face all those years ago.

Domi noticed the brass pitcher outside the bushes, a pitcher with a hole in the bottom. There couldn't be any water in it; every drop must have seeped out.

So when Malli came to the well and asked for a bucket of water to wash her feet, saying 'My tummy's aching,' Domi confronted her: 'What were you doing in the bushes?'

Turning coy, twisting and stretching her body languidly, Malli indicated that she hid in the bushes to answer nature's call. Then casting suspicious glances at the older woman, she went inside the house.

'Have you heard, Sana's mother,' Dā said, handing her a paan with thinly sliced areca nut. As she spoke, she remembered the heat of youth, the intoxication of stolen glances, the pairs of lovers from time immemorial. The Malli–Sautia pair was no different from the Sada–Domi pair. True, Domi's blood was not as passionate as before, but how could she have forgotten the past? Or was she experiencing a sense of frustration over her own failure? Was it the anger of the dead against the living? Domi didn't know and continued her story. 'Have you heard, Sana's mother?'

Sana's mother heard all Domi had to say. So did Gopalia, lying on a carpet and pretending to be fast asleep. Panting outside the door, the dog Banka did too.

Before an hour had passed, the eruption took place. The explosive had been ignited. Loud wailing, curses and words of abuse flowed freely. Tightening of towels and sari-ends around the waist, hurling of pots and pans, pushing and shoving, bodies thudding to the floor, blows landing on backs. The free use of brooms, nails and claws, hands and legs.

Dā

'Get out, old crone. Get the hell out, old witch. Get lost. No place for you in this household any longer.'

Dā was kicked out and her meagre possessions flung to the courtyard. She had always been possessive about her ramshackle box and her few saris. She cried bitterly as she picked them up one by one. A comb with several teeth missing lay under the eaves. She had brought it from her parents' place.

Pitch darkness, thicker than pot-black. An overcast sky. The trees and bushes resembling squatting mounds of darkness. A thin, winding, twisting strip of a path along the riverbank overlooking a sheer drop, running all the way to the rice-mill compound.

Dā puts the box down and sits upon it to catch her breath, the bundle of clothes clutched to her breast, her mouth tasting salty from the tears of her eyes, her body full of aches and pain; maybe a fever was coming on.

Waste—waste—waste.

My whole life's a waste.

God? He's deaf, just a stone. He's this beating, this the-hell-with-you attitude, this utter darkness.

All reduced to nothing, to mud.

Dā trembles as she pushes forward. This is the last time she'd sulk about in the world. One step after another. Into the water.

The mango grove, the gathering of dry leaves, the smiling face of Sada.

All noise, all sounds evaporating in the middle of the river, in the water that's nibbling away at the embankment on either side.

The waves lashing, chunks of earth falling off into the river.

A huge eerie silence.

Squatting on his haunches and beating his tail, Banka sets up a mournful wail: 'Bow-wow—ow—ow—ow . . .'

KANHU CHARAN MOHANTY

The Gnarled Sahada Tree

THIS HAPPENED IN Bikrampur, the place of Radha's life-long toil and eventual death. She was born as a daughter of Ichhapur and had become a daughter-in-law of Bikrampur. Situated on the banks of the river Bahuda, Bikrampur, hardly six miles from Ichhapur, was right on the border—in fact, the boundary line between the two provinces ran through the middle of the village. Innocent as she was of politics, Radha couldn't have cared less what province some towns were located in—whether Ichhapur and Vijayanagar were in Orissa, or Berhampur and Cuttack in Madras Presidency.

Radha's run-down house was in the middle of the village and the gnarled sahada tree that stood hard by the road in front had been the witness to the miseries that had befallen her in the last

---

'Mundi Sahada' is believed to have been written in 1936, the year Orissa became a separate province; the year of its first publication is uncertain.

The Gnarled Sahada Tree

twenty-five years. There were other witnesses too—the sand in the river, the hills beyond and, of course, her own two eyes.

Born to a farming family, she was married at fifteen. Her in-laws were not badly off then, their house not derelict and empty like today. On the contrary, it was quite a bustling place. In addition to her parents-in-law and her husband, her husband's younger brother and sister also lived there. The family owned several heads of bullocks, cows and buffaloes, goats and dogs; they had fields and farmland, orchards and barns.

Everyone in the family took to her, never mind that she didn't stand out either in looks or manner. Just about as dusky and robust as any other village belle, she was good at household chores and could work, ungrudging and untiring, from morning to night. Not one to fuss over food, she gladly ate whatever she got—whether rice or just rice-water and she came forward to lend a hand with whatever household work needed to be done. The welfare of the family was all she had in mind.

In all this time, the gnarled man-high sahada tree with its foliage of thick dark leaves remained the same as ever, neither growing nor decaying, vermilion dabbed all over its trunk in honour of Goddess Harapriya, who had taken up residence in it. The three-coned anthill, standing behind it like a miniature Mount Kailash, grew for six months a year and shrank during the next six months, especially in the monsoon. There was a hole at the base of the anthill, from which a cobra was often sighted crawling out to perambulate the holy tree. It could have been a great-great-great-great grandson of the primordial Snake Basuki, on whose head the earth rested.

Radha too had learnt to prostrate herself before the tree in obeisance since she came to the village as a daughter-in-law of the household. The Goddess was worshipped with great fanfare: drums were beaten, music played, fruits and milk offered.

In the following twenty-five years, Radha had witnessed these rituals being repeated on all occasions, both big and small, before or after an auspicious or inauspicious event. The Goddess had to be propitiated. No one could keep count of the goats, sheep and roosters sacrificed—their blood poured at the base of the tree. They could easily outnumber the leaves on the tree.

God knows what good all those animal sacrifices did for the villagers, but they did precious little good for Radha. From a nice dwelling, her house became a run-down hut; her hair turned grey, her teeth loosened, her skin lost its sheen, her body and mind hardened like the hills across the river. Her life became as dull and lustreless as the sandy expanse of the riverbed—arid, barren, useless.

In these twenty-five years, she had also been reduced from the daughter-in-law of a fairly well-to-do family to a poor day-labourer who had to go out and find some work or other. All her relatives on both sides of the family had died. She too had become like the gnarled sahada tree, but she still scrimped and saved for the future. For the future! She still had hope.

What a miserable history—the history of those twenty-five years. All those deaths in the family. Goats were sacrificed one after another before the Goddess. Their sacrificial blood, together with Radha's tears, had soaked the base of the gnarled sahada tree, but to no avail. Radha's prayers and entreaties fell on deaf ears; the Goddess was unmoved. Radha's relations departed, some of them in quite an untimely fashion. And the manner of their departure—well, what good would it do to get into all that? The fact is they all died.

Ten years down the line, only two persons were left—the two ill-fated daughters-in-law: Radha and her husband's younger brother's wife, Moti, a girl barely in her seventeenth year.

One year, the whole village was consumed by a fire. Many a house, among them Radha's, went up in flames. While the rest rebuilt their houses, Radha put up just two tiny rooms. What did she need a big house for? Who was there to inherit it?

Her father-in-law had taken a loan from Krishnamurthy, the goldsmith, to meet the wedding expenses of his two sons; the two sons had borrowed from Bishi Patra to meet the funeral expenses of their parents and the wedding charges for their sister. When her turn came, Radha went to Ram Patnaik and mortgaged the fields and farmland to meet, first the medical and then the funeral expenses of both her husband and his brother.

The goldsmith and the moneylenders had divided up the whole property among themselves, keeping an eye on the homestead. They hoped to share it equally one day when the two widows died.

Another ten years passed in the same dilapidated hut.

One night, Radha woke from sleep, eyes streaming, shaken by dreams of her trials and tribulations. Dreams of what she had actually lived through. She found she had fallen asleep with Moti's head in her lap.

As she gently ran her hand over Moti's head, the girl stirred. 'What's the matter, sister?'

'Dear Moti,' Radha said, grasping her hands. 'Don't take my words amiss, but I've been thinking about you. You must know the family property is all gone; nothing's left. You're still very young; why don't you remarry?'

Moti started and snatched her hands away.

Radha could fathom what was passing through the girl's mind. 'Please don't be angry with me, Moti. What I'm suggesting is only for your good. There're plenty of men sniffing around you, wishing to push you down into the muck, but none to stretch out their hands to pull you out of it. It hasn't escaped my notice that Krishnamurthy has been making nightly sorties.'

'What?' Moti hissed and snarled like a beaten snake. 'Finding fault with me? Are you a model of virtue and purity yourself, a lady of high morals?'

Radha clamped down her hand on Moti's mouth. 'Don't scream and shout. If you're angry and upset with me, come land some blows on my back, I'll gladly take them. I'm not blaming you one bit. Neither am I claiming to be a spotlessly virtuous woman myself. What I'm saying is from my own bitter experience, so listen closely to my suggestion. Every young woman dreams of becoming a mother some day. Women see darkness all around if they have no children. Don't think, dear Moti, that I'm blaming you for going after bodily pleasure. I had the same craving when I was younger. It's natural at your age. The good thing is, I'm still around here to protect you. When you remarry and move away, I'll surely be lonely, but satisfied too that I've found you happiness.'

Moti, stunned, fell into a long silence.

Outside, the summer moon blazed brightly in the silent night.

Shaking all over, Moti twirled her hands around Radha's neck, burying her face in her sister-in-law's bosom.

They both could hear someone clapping from under the shadows of the mango tree in the backyard.

Moti tightened her grip and said in a trembling voice, 'Sister, I'll do whatever you decide.'

Moti remarried and moved away to Nuapada.

Radha mortgaged the homestead.

Time passed.

Moti gave birth to a baby boy.

More time passed.

In all these years, Radha never once visited Moti in her new home. She was afraid the evil eye she was born under would destroy Moti's new life. She couldn't let that happen. Moti must live a long life of happiness and joy with her son and husband.

Moti sent her one request after another, but Radha turned them all down.

But after another seven years, Radha softened and paid Moti a visit. The two women hugged each other tightly and were drenched in tears. Radha drooled over Moti's seven-year-old son, Jatia, and couldn't stop petting him, fondly running her hand over the child's head, invoking the blessings of the Goddess on him. Before taking her leave, she surreptitiously tucked into Moti's hands what paltry sum she had saved over all these years.

A fortnight later, one evening, a messenger came running from Moti's place with the message that shook Radha to the very core of her being: grievously ill, Jatia was battling for his life. With unremitting high fever, eyes tightly shut, he was unconscious the whole time. Could Radha visit once again just to see the boy? It might do him immense good.

Radha promptly declined. Tell Moti, she advised the messenger, to pledge the child's life to the Goddess and keep praying. Radha's visit would do him no good.

The poor messenger had to hurry back the same night. The sky remained overcast, not a single star appeared. Nature was deathly still. The wind had stopped blowing.

By midnight, unable to sleep a wink, Radha tossed and turned; she was consumed by her thoughts. Why did she visit Moti in the first place? Why did she give in to the temptation she had resisted for so many years? What made her want to look her sister-in-law up? Why did she pet and fondle the little boy and run her hand over his head again and again? Why did she not remember that her love and affection was pure poison, which could only destroy the object of her adoration? Had anyone she loved survived? Would Jatia pull through? She had fawned over the child with such love, petted and fondled him; she had felt such a rush of love and affection for him! Would God take all that kindly? Would her prayers help now? Had they, in the past? How hard she had prayed! But had her prayers been answered even once? She had kept fasts and vigils night after night under the gnarled sahada tree, praying to the Goddess, hitting her head on the ground until it bled. But had the Goddess answered her prayers even once?

She had no doubt terrible news would come from Moti's place first thing in the morning. The news of Jatia's passing would be added to the string of bad news she had received in the past. How she would slump to the ground when she got the news, her body numb and mind deadened. How her hot tears had flowed in

The Gnarled Sahada Tree

torrents. How hunger had eventually won and she had gone out to find some work to earn a few wages to buy food.

She couldn't stem the tide of her anguish. But even as she was wracked by convulsive sobs, she decided she'd stop all prayers once and for all. Never again would she worship the Goddess. Never again would she venerate the sahada tree and call out to the Goddess. What had She ever done, how had She ever responded? Why should She be worshipped, offered food and water? Let Her go to hell. What more harm could She do when She had already done the worst? Why shouldn't she, Radha, take her revenge on Her? She might not have been able to take it out on mortals, but what prevented her from taking it out on Gods and Goddesses? It was time for her to wreak her vengeance. Let people say what they would, but Radha would retaliate against the tree-Goddess.

She sprang up and, groping in the dark, looked for something.

The dawn broke. The villagers thronged to the gnarled sahada tree.

Radha lay dead on the ground, her tongue sticking out. At the base of the tree lay an axe and from the cuts and slashes on the tree-trunk sap was oozing out.

On Radha's foot could be seen the signs of snakebite—tiny but unmistakable.

The Goddess had shown Her displeasure.

NITYANANDA MAHAPATRA

The Quest

The prince of Avanti, your majesty.'
   'Avanti, counsellor?'
   'Yes, my lord.'
   'When will the swayamvara take place?'
   'On the full moon day of Phalgun.'
   'How many days left?'
   'Eight months and ten days, your majesty.'

*

'How many did you say—three?'
   'Yes, your majesty. Three. Three gems.'
   'I see.'
   'The eldest daughters are exquisitely beautiful, but . . .'
   'Go on, counsellor.'

'Anweshan' was first published in 1938 in *Bhanja Pradeepa*, Vol. 7, No. 2.

The Quest

'The youngest is . . .'

'An ugly duckling, is she? That's all right. What do I care?'

*

'With all the riches in Kalinga's royal treasury, your majesty can buy heads but not hearts!'

'Money can buy both, counsellor. I'll show you yet.'

'With one-hundredth of his riches, the prince of Kalinga can buy thousands of slaves, but . . .'

'Go on.'

'With ten thousand times your entire wealth, O Prince of Kalinga, you cannot buy a single heart. Hearts are not up for sale, your majesty. Hearts are won, not bought. What does your majesty desire—a slave or a sweetheart?'

*

'Stuff and nonsense.'

'I humbly beg to disagree, your majesty.'

'You mean the prince of Kalinga cannot win the heart of a mere woman?'

'As a human being he can, but all his riches cannot.'

'Do you think the prince will have better luck with the princesses of Avanti if he goes to the swayamvara disguised as a beggar?'

'Your majesty must never confuse love with infatuation. Infatuation withers. Love endures.'

*

The youth was handsome, with a broad chest, long arms, large eyes and a broad forehead, but was dressed in tattered rags. Whoever saw him in the streets of Avanti felt pity for him.

In Avanti, resplendent with palaces, riches, invincible and swashbuckling cavaliers astride handsome horses, begging was an evil dream—a crime.

*

'So then, young beggar!'

'At your command, your majesty.'

'Didn't you know that begging is an offence in this land?'

'I did, your majesty.'

'Are you ready for the sentence?'

'Yes, your majesty.'

'The punishment is harsh.'

'What can be worse than begging, my lord?'

'So you hate to beg?'

'With all my heart.'

'It pleases us to hear that. But the law is the law. You are sentenced to eight months of solitary confinement. But since you abhor begging and perhaps were led to it by circumstances beyond your control, you shall be allowed one small privilege of your choice during your imprisonment. Name it.'

'I am grateful to your majesty for this act of kindness. I pray for your eternal well-being.'

'You can state your wish.'

'May I be allowed out of my cell for a while every evening, to play my flute.'

The Quest

'For how long?'
'An hour or so, my lord.'
'Granted.'

*

Not far from the royal palace stood the prison—a cluster of narrow pigeonholes, built of stone, with a high wall around them. There were no windows; only a tiny hole below the roof in every cell to let in a little air. The heavy iron gates closed like the bloodthirsty jaws of a monster.

Every evening, the young beggar came out of his cell, sat on a large stone in the courtyard and planted a warm lingering kiss on his flute.

Every evening, the palace trembled with the liquid melody of his music. Cuckoos trilled out of season; the still waters of the crystal-clear bathing pools broke into gentle ripples. And in the remote recesses of the royal chambers, the princesses' hearts beat uncontrollably.

*

'Prisoner!'
 'Yes.'
 'Where are you from?'
 'Kalinga.'
 'Who gave you this flute?'
 'The prince of Kalinga.'
 'The prince himself?'
 'Yes.'

'I hear he's very handsome.'
'As handsome as Lord Kartikeya.'
'Will he come to the swayamvara?'
'He may or he may not.'

*

'Prisoner!'
   'Yes.'
   'Are you from Kalinga?'
   'That's right.'
   'Who taught you to play the flute?'
   'The prince of Kalinga.'
   'The prince?'
   'Yes.'
   'I hear he's extremely rich.'
   'Even richer than Kuber.'
   'Will he come to the swayamvara?'
   'He may or he may not.'

*

'Stranger!'
   'Who's that?'
   'Are you from Kalinga?'
   'Yes, I am.'
   'Oh, stranger!'
   'Yes?'
   'Can you tell me . . .?'
   'Tell you what?'

The Quest

'Something...'

'Ask.'

'Why does your heart echo through the notes of a little bamboo flute?'

The prisoner started and tried in vain to see the questioner in the deepening gloom.

'Stranger!'

'Yes?'

'Does the prince of Kalinga play the flute as hauntingly?'

'Even more hauntingly.'

'Is he kind?'

'Very.'

'And learned?'

'Like Lord Ganesh.'

'And brave, too?'

'Like Arjun.'

'Will he... will he come to the swayamvara at Avanti?'

'He may or he may not.'

*

There where sunflowers wilted by the prison walls, when the deepening dusk hid the rough contours of the monstrous stone edifice and the sky shivered with the tremulous notes of the prisoner's flute—a young woman was seen to appear for a brief while and then disappear. And so it went on for many days.

*

On the other side of the prison, where the night flowers spread their intoxicating fragrance, where the great green bowl of the earth and the diabolical dome of the prison mingled in the darkness and the lilting notes of a flute twirled through the pastures of the sky—another young woman, shorter than the first, appeared and then disappeared. And so it went on for many days.

*

When, in the hushed silence of a late evening, a light breeze stirred within the prison, the frail figure of a young woman stole into the courtyard with a bowl of fruit and placed it before the prisoner's cell.

'Who's there?' the prisoner asked.

'Someone.'

The prisoner ate the fruit and the young woman collected the bowl and disappeared. They never saw or spoke to each other and only the darkness saw their eyes swimming with tears. And so it went on for many days.

*

The evening before the full moon of Phalgun.

The following day, the swayamvara for the three princesses of Avanti would be held. The same day, the prisoner would be freed.

'Prisoner, play your flute.'

'The flute shall play no longer.'

'Why?'

'For eight long months I played my flute. People stopped to listen. But, but . . .'

'But what?'

'But I could never touch the heart of the woman I played for. Maybe she was thrilled to hear me play, but she could never divine the anguish in my heart. She did not respond because I'm a beggar and a prisoner and she a princess.'

'A princess?'

'Yes, a princess of Avanti.'

'Of Avanti?'

'Yes. Did that startle you?'

'What insolence! As a lowly beggar, you aspire for the most exquisite flower in the land? Don't you know the grand swayamvara for the princesses of Avanti will be held tomorrow and princes from other lands will gather here to try their luck? Perhaps the prince of Kalinga will win the princess.'

'Maybe.'

'One word from me and you'll be sent to the gallows.'

'I couldn't care less. Of what use is *my* life to me?'

'Very well! Know then that I'm the eldest princess of Avanti.'

*

'Stranger, why is your flute silent?'

'The flute shall play no longer.'

'But why?'

'I broke it.'

'Why did you do that?'

'There was so little appreciation.'

'Far from it. Many people stopped to listen.'

'But no one understood what my flute was crying out for.'

'How do you know?'

'I asked myself.'

'Did you care to explain to your audience?'

'I cared a lot and for far too long.'
'How long?'
'One day less than eight months.'
'But who is it you played your flute for?'
'The person I pine for.'
'Who is that precious person?'
'I dare not say.'
'Go ahead, I'll keep it a secret.'
'She's a princess of Avanti.'
'What—a princess of Avanti?'
'Did that startle you?'
'Impudent fool! You're a dwarf and you aspire for the moon! How dare you fall in love with a princess of Avanti, who might adorn the throne of Kalinga tomorrow? Do you know what would happen to you if I reported you?'

'Death holds no fear for me.'

'Very well! You had better be ready for it. And know that I am the second princess of Avanti.'

*

'Traveller!'
'Yes?'
'Why didn't you eat today?'
'Hunger has forsaken me.'
'But why?'
'No food can satiate the hunger of the heart.'
'Why aren't you playing your flute?'
'The flute played for only one person.'

'Isn't that lucky person here this evening to listen to it?'
'She hears but doesn't listen.'
'How do you know?'
'I asked myself.'
'Stranger, is the heart of a princess a stone?'
'Yes, like a gem, a stone—hard and cold.'
'She sees nothing?'
'Only the outside.'
'Not the mind?'
'Not the mind but the wealth.'
'Can she not fathom the sorrow of others?'
'No, only her *own* happiness.'
'You're wrong.'

*

'Prisoner!'
'Who's that?'
'Sush, keep your voice low.'
'Why should a man condemned to death fear his voice will be heard?'
'For heaven's sake keep your voice down. If you wish to live, do as I say.'
'But I've no wish to live.'
'Oh no, you *must* live.'
'For whom?'
'For someone.'
'Who's that someone?'
'There's no time to explain everything. The prison doors are open and you'll find a horse outside. Please get away from here as

fast as the wind, otherwise tomorrow morning you will have to go to the gallows.'

'But who are you and why have you come to set me free?'

'No time to go into all that. I may only say that I'm carrying out the orders of someone who has looked into your soul and suffered your sorrows.'

'I can't thank that person enough. But may I know who this mysterious *someone* is?'

'I am not allowed to tell you. All I can say is that the haunting notes of your flute have touched *her* deeply.'

'So it's a woman! But she never asked me to play my flute!'

'She didn't.'

'I decline the offer. It's not fitting for a son of Kalinga to steal away in the dark of night. But please tell me who this woman is who's been so kind to me.'

'Would you believe me if I told you?'

'Why not?'

'Are you sure?'

'Of course!'

'She ... she ...'

'Oh, stop torturing me.'

'She's the youngest princess of Avanti.'

*

The day of the swayamvara.

'Your majesty!'

'At your command, Prince of Kalinga!'

'Your first and second daughters have hung their garlands on my statue, not on me. When I was a prisoner ...'

'Forgive them their follies, prince. They didn't recognize you.'

'Neither did your youngest daughter. Lord of Avanti, I might be a rich and mighty king, but for those eight months in your prison I was the lowliest beggar in your land. The young woman who could fall for such a wretch . . . Well, she alone shall be my queen. Give us your blessings.'

HARISCHANDRA BADAL

The Tiger

On RETURNING HOME from work, Ramesh, the experienced treasurer-in-charge at the Collectorate, hung his walking stick in its place, folded and put away his shawl and growled in a big booming voice from under his thick bushy moustache in evident self-importance: 'Pra-bha!'

His eight-year-old daughter, Prabha, who had just taken a big bite of the raw mango she had scrounged from her best friend, Baula, quickly transferred the fruit to her left hand, hid it in the folds of her sari and came out on the run. 'Oh, you're home, father!' With her mouth full of the sweet and sour fruit, her voice sounded muffled.

Noticing how agitated she was, Ramesh became grave. 'What have you been up to, girl? How come you're not speaking as clearly as usual?'

Although little Prabha had only sixteen teeth—just half the number an adult can have—she worked them like an electric

---

'Bagha' was first published in 1939 in *Sahakar*, Vol. 10, No. 7

sharpener, cutting and grinding; even sixty-four teeth couldn't have performed better. In the few seconds it took her father to fire his question, she swallowed and answered in her usual sharp, clear voice, 'What have I been up to, huh, father? Why, nothing, nothing at all! Didn't I come running as soon as I heard you?'

But her father, who had not been a treasurer-in-charge at the Collectorate for a very long time for nothing, had four eyes instead of two and couldn't be taken in by a mere slip of a girl. Fixing her with a stern look, he enquired: 'All right, where in the blazes is Ghana?'

Ghana, short for Ghanashyam, was his seven-year-old son. A holy terror, if ever there was one, he was adept at clambering up high trees and walls; bullying kids many years older than him with threats and beatings; stealing pickles, preserves and sweets from home and books, notebooks and pencils from school. His finesse in these matters had to be seen to be believed. He did not give two hoots for his mother, elder sister, uncles and aunts. He withstood even the floggings at school like Casabianca, the heroic boy on the burning deck. The only person in the whole world he was mortally afraid of was his father; in his presence, he metamorphosed into a meek and mild lamb—as sweet, quiet and gentle as they come. So superb was his acting that often the father would hurl the upraised cane—meant for brisk use on the boy's back—at a passing tomcat or some other thing. The little monster was the scourge of his mother, but one word from his father could petrify him. When Ramesh was around, the boy's voice would drop into a sweet, sibilant whisper as he begged his mother: 'Ma, give me some rice puffs and jaggery balls to eat. I'm famished.'

The boy's first brush with the Odia alphabet took place when he turned five. The abadhan, or traditional teacher, put a piece of chalk in his right hand ceremonially and, after receiving his customary fees and gifts, left the boy's future learning to his mother. It was she who helped the boy to practise the letters: *a, aa* . . . *ka, kha* . . . and the rest. Prabha, his older sibling, was made to learn the lessons with him.

When he had mastered the letters *pa, pha, ba, bha, ma*, Ghana began to read, haltingly, the words in his picture book. Underneath the picture of the tiger, he could make out the letters *baa* and *gha*. Never having seen a baagha tiger—such a strange animal—he turned to his mother: 'Ma, tell us, what kind of an animal this is.'

She tried to describe it as best as she could. Called the big cat, the tiger was a ferocious predator with sharp teeth and claws, had a big bushy moustache and tremendous speed and strength. Then she told the children many bone-chilling tales, including the one about the tiger and the jackal.

Listening to his mother and staring at the picture, Ghana found a similarity between a tiger and a cat. 'Is the tiger something like the wild, unruly tomcat of ours, Ma? Perhaps the cat is the tiger's uncle and the tiger is a cat too.'

The child's observations made his mother laugh. His sister joined in, although she hadn't the faintest idea what the joke was about. Ghana's stinging slap across her face took her unawares. More slaps and blows would have followed had their mother not intervened just in time. Prabha burst out bawling and would have gone on and on, but just then they heard from outside: 'Pra-bha!'

'Hush,' their mother said. 'Stop bawling. The tiger's home.'

The Tiger

Ghana jumped out of his skin. 'Where's the tiger, Ma, where is it?'

Forgetting to cry, Prabha too scanned the front courtyard with tear-filled eyes.

The boy was about to repeat his question when the distraught mother clamped her hand on his mouth. 'Hush, hush! The tiger's here. Not a squeak now.'

The next moment, they were able to see Ramesh in the doorway. His stern gaze swept over them all, and he growled: 'Who was creating that godawful racket—Ghana? This place is worse than a fish market.'

Ghana had already turned into a mouse and Prabha, fearing her father's ire might swing to her, had her nose buried in her lessons: '*Ba re aakar baa* . . .'

Stroking his bushy moustache, Ramesh ordered his wife: 'I want to talk to you. Come to the next room.' Without waiting for her reply, he walked off to the adjoining room, his wooden clogs clattering on the floor.

Prabha read the word aloud again: '*Baa* and *gha* is Baagha. Tiger.'

Before Sarada could join her husband, she heard the plaintive crying of her youngest child. The little thing was up. So, instead of reporting to her lord and master right away, she hurried to the inner quarters to pick up the child from the bed, sopping wet from his own pee and nursed him. As she was making a fresh bed for the baby, she heard the clatter of clogs again. It stopped outside the door.

'Didn't you hear me? Didn't I make myself clear? I wanted to talk to you!'

'The baby woke up and was crying. I had to nurse him. Let him have some milk first; then I will come to you.'

'Babies and more babies! Ugh, this brood. A bawling, crawling, mewling, fighting bunch. But are you the only harassed mother on earth?'

'Good grief, they aren't just one or two, but seven! One too many for anyone to take care of! And the baby being breastfed is not even a year old!' Sarada cried out. But her feeble protest fell on deaf ears. What else could the poor woman do? Putting the child down on the bed with a deep sigh, she followed her husband.

'Look,' he said airily. 'I've invited a few people for lunch tomorrow. They're all my childhood friends from Narsinghpur. I want the spread to be spectacular—fish, meat, pilaf and sweet porridge, the works. Nothing must go awry.'

'Tomorrow's Thursday and a holy ekadashi into the bargain,' she protested. 'Fish and meat will not be available in the market. You better send word to the fishermen's colony to deliver their morning catch to our doorstep. As for meat, better buy a kid goat . . . But who's going to cook and serve fish and meat dishes tomorrow?'

He brushed her aside. 'Will people have to go without fish and meat tomorrow because of your observance of ekadashi and Thursday? Forget your inhibitions, observances and prohibitions, fasts and vigils, forget your no-fish no-meat superstitions. Make proper arrangements for tomorrow exactly as I've ordered.'

With these words, he walked off into the drawing room to lie back in his reclining chair and enjoy his hookah. Soon the tobacco pipe began to gurgle—*bhudur, bhudur, bhudur*. The rings of smoke that spiraled up made the domestic atmosphere heavier.

The Tiger

Although the epitome of patience, Sarada fumed. The strain of looking after the family day in and day out was getting to her and now, on top of it all, instead of words of sympathy and appreciation, she was being humiliated.

Prabha and Ghana were in the middle of a massive argument.

'Tigers eat humans,' Prabha said, shaking her head sagely.

'Have you seen that with your own eyes?' Ghana mocked her.

But Prabha wouldn't back down. Wasn't she the older of the two and therefore wiser? She raised her voice. 'I tell you, tigers eat humans.'

'You fool, how can a tiger eat a human?' He brandished his wooden sword. 'If ever a tiger comes anywhere near me, I'll split its skull in two with one stroke of my sword.'

'You numbskull,' Prabha laughed derisively. 'Don't you remember what Ma was saying the other day? There was once a king who went into the forest to hunt. He had elephants, horses and hundreds of men armed with bows and arrows, guns and spears and lances. A tiger began to stalk them, hiding behind the bushes and at the first opportunity, it made off with a man. It happened in the blink of an eye, so fast that the king's men could do nothing. They searched but failed to find hide or hair of either the tiger or the man.'

'What does that prove? Nothing!'

'The tiger ate the man and went back to its cave in the depths of the forest.'

'And who filled you in on all this—the tiger himself? I tell you, the man killed the tiger.' Prabha was infuriated. How the boy was bragging! As if he was a fearless fellow himself! 'Ma said a tiger kills humans and you're saying just the opposite?'

'Of course!' Ghana thrust out his chest and crowed, sensing victory.

But Prabha still wouldn't give up. 'The tiger killed the man, but the king's men didn't find his remains.'

'The tiger might have dragged him off to some remote spot.'

'The whole forest was searched. The king was determined to run the beast to the ground and have its head chopped off.'

That caught Ghana short.

It was Prabha's turn to let out a snort of laughter. 'As I said, you're one big fool. Tigers eat humans. Can Ma ever be wrong?'

Ghana was stubborn not only when it came to dishing out blows and slaps but also when it came to sticking to his views and opinion. 'Don't talk big like a little Miss Know-It-All. The king's entourage might have been large and strong, with elephants, horses, expert hunters and what not, but still the tiger could spirit away a man. Wouldn't that be humiliating—to snatch a man from under your nose? So who would the king be angry with—the tiger or the man? He would have ordered the man's head to be cut off for being such a fool. That must have been the reason why the poor man didn't get back to the king to report his kill.'

'Ma,' Prabha began to shriek in anger, making a dash for the kitchen, where their mother was busy with her chores. 'Ma, listen to Ghana. He's being a brat and insisting that the man killed the tiger but didn't dare to report it because the king would be angry . . .'

Their mother had finished frying the first batch of fish and was preparing to cook the meat curry, when her daughter tugged at her hand and repeated her complaint.

'Oh, these children!' she shouted, jerking her hand free. 'They'll be the death of me. How does one cope with them? And their

The Tiger

father is such a tartar he wants every wish of his carried out to the letter and threatens me if so much as a pinch of lime is missing from his betel leaf! And here's his darling daughter pestering me with inane questions! Be off, girl.'

Prabha, who had hoped their mother would take her side, found herself crushed. Her heart was broken and convulsive sobs began to rise inside her. But she clamped down on them, although she couldn't help the tears that streamed down her cheeks in torrents.

Moved at the sight of the distraught girl, Sarada set aside her chores for the moment and rushed to hug and comfort her. 'Poor thing, come to Ma. Come and tell me what the boy did to upset you.' Her voice was so soft and loving that Prabha broke down.

'Ma, Ghana said tigers don't eat humans.'

Watching them from the doorway, Ghana realized he had to make a move if he hoped to be one up. 'But Ma,' he said in a sudden burst of inspiration, 'do you remember what Uncle said the other day? He said tigers don't eat humans. They only rip their hearts out and suck their blood.'

Who knew whether their uncle had indeed come out with something like this, but Ghana could concoct anything when it suited him.

But when he found their mother keeping quiet, he grew agitated. 'Tigers don't eat up humans, do they, Ma?'

'That's right,' Sarada said as if in a spell. 'Tigers don't eat humans. They only rip their hearts out and suck their blood.'

Prabha and Ghana were so surprised they looked at each other in silence.

The angry spluttering of the fish frying in the oil woke Sarada from the spell. Wiping her daughter's face as well as her own, she picked up a spoon and stirred the pot. 'Go now, my dears. Go and play.'

Prabha and Ghana slunk away as if chastised.

Noon. Lunch time. The servant Rama went to the drawing room to inform Ramesh. 'Lunch is served in the dining room, sir.'

Laughing and joking, Ramesh led his friends into the inner quarters. Rama followed behind, but before the guests could reach the dining room, he scuttled off to fetch fresh towels. That made Ramesh fly into a rage. 'Where are you off to, you rascal? You haven't poured water for my guests to wash their hands!'

The outburst petrified the poor servant.

The Brahmin cook of the house, Banshidhar, served lunch and respectfully retreated into the kitchen.

Putting a piece of fried fish into his mouth, Ramesh made a face and summoned the cook. 'Banshi!'

The cook rushed back; anxiety writ large on his face. The master's grave expression scared him out of his wits.

'What's the matter with you, Banshi?' Ramesh exploded, his voice hitting a higher octave. 'You don't like the work here any more? You're sick of it, are you? What have you served—fried fish or burnt fish?'

'Sir!'

'Don't sir me. You should have been careful, especially when I've invited guests. But you seem to have taken leave of your senses. I think you're no longer fit to work here.'

'Sir, I cooked only the vegetarian dishes because today's ekadashi,' the cook replied. 'The mistress herself fried the fish and cooked the mutton dishes.'

'What, the mistress cooked the fish and meat?'

'Yes, sir.'

'But has the mistress become Her Highness Madam Governor that she can fry the fish until they're burnt?'

From behind the curtain, Sarada overheard every bit of their conversation.

Luckily, one of the guests intervened. 'Why, Ramesh, the fish fry is absolutely fine. There's nothing wrong with it. Doesn't taste bad at all. Maybe the piece you got was slightly overdone. Come on, man, the hostess has done an excellent job. Can't find any fault. On the contrary, the mutton pilaf is simply divine. As delicious as fragrant . . . Cook, will you please serve me another helping? And yes, you may serve Shyam some more mutton curry too.'

The harangue about the fish fry died down; it was back to laughing, joking and chatting cheekily among the friends. Before the lunch was over, Rama hurried to put the tray of fragrant paan in the drawing room and prepare the master's hookah.

Lunch over, Ramesh and his friends retired to the drawing room for a roll of the dice. Then, remembering he had left the set—pieces, cloth board and all—in the inner quarters, he went back.

Sarada who was looking for an opportunity to collar her husband, mustered courage the moment he emerged with the set. 'Good grief, how could you humiliate me so badly before your friends? I can take the insults you so generously dole out in private, but to strip me of my self-respect before outsiders . . . ah, what must they have thought of me . . . chhi, chhi, the shame of it!'

'What rubbish!' Ramesh barked, his voice dripping with sarcasm. 'Just because I found fault with the fish fry? Was that such a big blow? But why couldn't you have been more careful? Instead of finding fault with yourself, you dare find fault with me?'

Stroking his moustache and puffing his chest out, he headed back to the drawing room, his clogs clattering away most gratingly. As he passed the kitchen, Banshi shrank away in the the doorway, but Ramesh chose not to notice.

After he was out of sight, Banshi came to Sarada. 'Mistress, come and eat something. It's quite late.'

'Oh Banshi,' Sarada said. 'Go and eat something yourself. I'm not feeling well and will skip lunch.' The cook was about to say something, but she shut the door on him.

Poor Banshi, he knew why the mistress had chosen to miss lunch. His eyes lingered on the closed door for a long while. As he went back to the kitchen, he muttered under his breath: 'The wretch, the scum, he made his poor wife go without a morsel of food.' Of course, there was no one to hear his words.

Sarada, her face drained of blood, slumped on her bed. She was dog tired; her mind was in a turmoil. Then she overheard Prabha and Ghana carrying on with their quarrel in the backyard.

'Oh yes,' Ghana was saying. 'That's exactly what Uncle was saying. I heard him with my own ears.'

'Oh, come on!' Prabha was dismissive. 'You're a born liar.'

Ghana flew into a rage. Being called a liar was the worst insult and he couldn't bear it. 'What did you say, you witch? You are the liar—you, you!'

'Go on you-you-ing all you want. I'm going to cross-check with Uncle when he comes.'

'So go ahead and find out for yourself whether I'm lying...' the boy piped up. 'All right, let's assume I'm telling lies, but did you not hear with your own ears what Ma said earlier this morning?

Didn't she say that a tiger doesn't eat humans, it only plucks their heart and drinks their blood?'

Sarada felt as if somebody was plucking her heart and drinking her blood. 'Ah!' She could hear no more. Clutching her heart with her hands she sank on the bed in a dead faint.

GODAVARISH MAHAPATRA
Maguni's Bullock Cart

KHALIKOTE, WITH ABOUT two hundred thousand people, had its inevitable share of both births and deaths. The news, however, never travelled beyond the confines of families and neighbourhoods. But when Maguni died, the news spread throughout the town and beyond. Whoever heard it, exclaimed after a stunned silence, 'Oh, the poor fellow's gone! How sad!'

Who was Maguni? The ruler of Khalikote? The king of a neighbouring state? A major figure in the administration? A big taxpayer, a rich moneylender? A Congress leader spearheading the Satyagraha movement for independence, delivering stirring speeches to delirious crowds? An acclaimed patriot? Or a prominent citizen who was always chosen to receive visiting dignitaries? Who was he? Why did everyone in the town as well as in the far-flung villages on the forest's edge know who he was?

Maguni was not an important man. All he ever did to eke out a living was to drive a bullock cart. He had struggled all his life,

---

'Magunira Sagada' was first published in 1939 in *Nav Bharat*, Vol. 6, No. 6.

Maguni's Bullock Cart

not for his country or countrymen, but simply for himself, for his own survival. Yet the bond he had forged with his pair of bullocks left a lasting impression on people's minds.

Every day, Maguni made his trip to the railway station, as regular as the sun that rose and set over the town. He was as punctual as a clock, people said. In the rainy months, when the sun remained hidden behind clouds, his passage announced the time of day. The seasons could be irregular, the monsoons delayed, or the summer not hot enough, but never did a day go by without Maguni's cart rumbling along the road. Even on bitterly cold winter mornings, when people sat in their verandas wrapped in blankets, Maguni drove his cart along the serpentine road beneath the hills with a song on his lips.

So what if the king of Khalikote had two motorcars, Maguni sometimes joked, did the king have a driver like him? His bullock cart was far better than any motorcar. He just had to gently pat Kalia and Kasara on their rumps to rev up the engine and belt out snatches of the popular ballad *'Rama and Laeekhana followed the trail of the magic deer...'* to make the bullocks fly. The song echoed through the hills, waking up the birds and animals. Forest pheasants called and stray village dogs howled as his cart inexorably rolled by.

Criss-crossing the entire length and breadth of the town and beyond, he kept people hooked on the stories of his life, which flowed from his mouth in an endless stream. Raised with love and care by doting parents, his had been a wonderful childhood: a comfortable bed, copious meals, not having to do a day's work. Life continued to treat him well even after both his parents died and he grew to manhood. He married a beautiful girl, whose words were as sweet as her lips. Her breath was fragrance itself and flowers bloomed where she walked. Life was a dream, a glorious riot of happiness and joy. Only this didn't last long. His young wife departed for the other world, where he hoped to join her when his days were done.

These poignant stories brought tears not only to the eyes of listeners but also to his own. Discreetly wiping his tears, he would change the subject and talk of something else. The journey would come to an end but not his stories. With the solitary exception of the king of Khalikote, everyone—from the dewan to the managers, from lawyers and moneylenders to the followers of Mahatma Gandhi—had boarded his cart at one time or another. His cart had witnessed so much: young widows on their heart-breaking journeys from their in-laws back to their parents; merry brides riding joyously from their parents' home to their husbands'; Gada Raul of Mandal village, jailed for failure to pay his taxes and whose worldly possessions, down to his last broom, were transported to the king's court in this cart; or Madhu Rath of Bendalia, sent to prison for committing a murder; prosecution lawyers; handcuffed peasant leaders courting arrest with a smile on their faces. Maguni's cart had seen sorrow, it had seen joy. Torrents of tears had drenched its straw seats just as bursts of laughter had rattled its bamboo ribcage. So when Maguni spoke, a legend spoke, the living voice of Khalikote's history spoke. He brought so much gusto and excitement to his stories that even the bullocks at times slowed down and stopped. 'Look how these animals love to listen to my stories,' he'd chuckle. He never used the goad on them.

But the day came when Maguni learnt that people were to have another means of transport. The wealthy Singhs were planning to

Maguni's Bullock Cart

put a bus on the road. He broke into uproarious laughter. A bus to beat his well-nourished Kalia–Kasara team? Would people ever desert his cart for a god-forsaken bus?

Everyone laughed at him, but he was unperturbed.

A few days later, a monster of a motorbus rolled into town.

Poor Maguni's done for, people remarked. Now his business will fold. How can a bullock cart ever match a bus that can carry twenty people at a time and cover forty miles in an hour?

Maguni's heart sank and panic seized him. True, he did not break down and cry, but he came close to tears. He remembered the public meeting at Kodola he had once driven past. A speaker there had asserted that machines were no match for human hands. If that was true, then wasn't his bullock cart better than a motorbus? He'd go and appeal to all those people who had attended the meeting and listened to the speech. Would they turn a deaf ear to him? If they did, then he'd go to their leader, Mahatma Gandhi. Everyone said he was a great friend of the poor and wretched of the earth. Would he too turn Maguni away? Would he let Maguni perish and the Singhs prosper?

The bus plied the same route as Maguni's cart. Day after day after day the bus went full, the cart empty.

Maguni rose at midnight to go and park his cart in front of the railway station before daybreak, but the passengers chose to wait for the bus, which arrived late in the morning.

He changed the old upholstery of his straw seats for new jute sacking, but people still headed for the bus.

He took passengers by the hand, to lead them to his cart, but they all headed for the bus.

Days passed and then some more.

Maguni stuck it out. He cut down his meals from two to one a day.

A few days more and Maguni switched from hot, freshly cooked rice to watered rice.

More days passed and Maguni went from a single helping of watered rice a day to one every two days.

Still more days; he did not light his hearth for days on end, as there was nothing to cook.

Kalia and Kasara became woefully thin. Their ribs jutted out. Often, Maguni put his arms around their necks and the three of them wept silent tears.

Gone off his hinges, people commented, crazy from hunger and grief.

More days went by.

Then came the morning when people had to break down the door of Maguni's house to get to his body. He lay lifeless on a tattered mattress, his goad beneath it.

A pyre was lit for him. Thick black smoke billowed into the sky and countless birds, flapping their wings in anguish, flew by. The news swept the town and nearly two hundred thousand people lamented, 'Oh, poor Maguni's gone! What a pity!'

SATCHIDANANDA ROUTRAY

Flower of Evil

Jagu Tiadi—an opium-addict, lusty drummer and undisputed leader of the Brahmin kirtan singers of Podabasant village—had made a name for himself as a cremator. When it came to burning a body, there was no one, even in the neighbouring villages, who could rival him.

Corpses, you see, can cause plenty of headaches: some slowpokes refuse to catch fire; others, as sly in death as in life, suddenly thrust out a stiff hand or leg, upsetting the carefully arranged pyre; some burst open at the seams at the slightest heat and their abundant body fluids douse the fire. Only a few go without a fuss. Faced with such difficulties, pallbearers would look to Jagu for help and advice. Fighting off sleep and an opium-induced languor, he would struggle to his feet, take out a smoking log and land a couple of hefty blows on the unyielding corpse. 'Go quickly, or I'll hand you a second death,' he would curse, as he saw to it that the skull

---

'Masanira Phula' was first published in 1939 in *Aarati*, Vol. 1, No. 2.

was smashed to smithereens, the legs broken into splinters, the stomach deflated like a pricked balloon and the body caught fire and turned to ashes.

Until it was all over, Jagu would lumber about the cremation ground littered with ash-heaps, winnowing-fans, broomsticks, shards, rags and knotted balls of hair and nails. A smooth cremation never failed to warm his heart. 'Thank God,' he would say, slapping oil on his thighs for the mandatory ritual dip in the village pond. 'There, that's a decent corpse for you.'

When cholera and smallpox struck the village and almost every home had a body to cremate, Jagu was naturally in great demand. If a family tried to reduce his fee by so much as a paisa, he would leave the body to rot in the house. He would not budge an inch unless he was paid a quarter-rupee coin and a tola each of ganja and opium. These, of course, were in addition to the customary offering of rice, new clothes and invitations to three funeral feasts.

For Jagu, the death of a married woman while her husband was still alive was nothing less than a bonanza. If she belonged to a prosperous family, Jagu was entitled to her gold nose-stud or earrings; if she came from a humbler home, he took her silver toe-rings. Before placing the body on the pyre, he himself would remove the jewellery. Sometimes, when the piece did not come off easily, Jagu would impatiently yank it off; if in the process the corpse bled, that did not upset him in the least. Why, he never even hesitated to strip a dead woman just to make sure he had not missed out on anything valuable.

He rejoiced most in the death of a pregnant woman, or better still, a death during childbirth. On such occasions, he would refuse to lift the bier unless he was paid a full rupee. People who haggled with him were damned; he would have nothing to do with the cremation. He could even talk the other pallbearers into a strike. But once he got his silver coin, he would get on with the job with the proficiency of a professional. Belting out lusty shouts in praise of God to the rhythmic beat of drums, he would dance down the village path, his spotless white sacred-thread girdling his black-as-granite body. His big booming voice, echoing through the village, scared the little children off the road. At the cremation ground, once the washerman had slit open the swollen belly of the dead woman, he would pluck the foetus out. Sometimes he beat the half-formed child into a pulp before unceremoniously throwing it into the fire. No one dared comment upon his outrageous behaviour. After all, there was no one more efficient than Jagu to deal with the dead!

The relish with which Jagu often described his exploits left no one in doubt about the pride he took in his calling. 'Who kept Narasingh Mishra's wife's pyre going in the pouring rain? Who found the way to reduce Nath Brahma to cinders when the bloated-up old bounder was a wet mass?' he would ask. Even when cremations took a long time and were tiresome, Jagu would linger patiently until the end, sometimes just about the only person around. And the nether world notables he encountered on these ungodly occasions! There was the Headless One roosting at the fringe of the Seven Tree grove; the old witch in the crotch of a mango tree by the Muktajhar stream roasting a newborn baby over a pale cold fire. Pausing only for a deep drag on the chillum to clear his throat, he reeled off his stories so vividly that the listeners in the village bhagavatghara, covered in goose flesh, huddled closer to each other.

One late evening in the month of Ashwin, when the sky hung low with dark clouds, Jagu sat on his veranda, nursing a splitting headache. He had a muffler around his head, his temples smeared with dabs of quicklime. The village priest was reading aloud the holy Harivamsa. Suddenly, a loud wail pierced the stillness of the evening. Somebody had died. Jagu grew restless, wondering who it was. Soon someone who had gone to the shop at the other end of the village brought the news. It was the young wife Jatia had deserted. Jagu sat up. Here was a big chance for a shiny silver coin. Not often in this sinful world did women predecease their poor husbands. It did not matter that Jatia had long since abandoned his wife.

His joy, however, was short-lived. According to the grapevine, the young woman was pregnant and that the local abortionist's potion had brought on her death. Jagu realized he could cremate her only at the risk of excommunication.

All Jatia's old mother had been left with in the world was this young daughter-in-law and now she too had died in the most disgraceful of circumstances. Jatia had left home three years ago to seek his fortune in Calcutta and had broken all ties with his family. The rumour had spread that he had taken another wife. Abandoned by her son and now by her daughter-in-law, Jatia's mother rolled in the dust, bewailing her fate.

Although the village elders blamed the old woman for not keeping a strict eye on her daughter-in-law, this was no longer her private misfortune. If the police got to know about it, it would be a slur on the honour of her caste and on the village as well. The body had to be disposed of as quickly as possible, for there was no lack of snitches in the village to carry tales to the police. Jatia's mother felt so mortified that she held a straw between her toothless gums and prostrated herself before the village elders.

A few young men volunteered to cart the corpse to the cremation ground. Straw ropes were plaited, a bamboo bier was readied and the winnowing fans, broomsticks, pots and their slings were collected from inside the house. The dead woman was wrapped in a sari and tied down to a bier. The cremation seemed far from a tame affair: the rains threatened to come at any moment and if the police arrived before it was over, the whole village could be thrown in the dock. Urgent summons were sent to Jagu.

But Jagu would have none of it. The young woman had died in sin and he did not wish to pollute himself by cremating her. Jagu found his moral qualms too strong to be overcome—until an offer of five big silver coins was made; it was only then that he reluctantly accepted the assignment.

Jatia's mother dug out her nest egg from a hole in the wall, but it was barely enough for the wood, kerosene, rice and fees for the barber and washerman. So would Jagu kindly relent and have the gold piece the dead woman wore on her nose?

'Jai Hari.' Jagu turned to the pallbearers. 'Praise Hari. Ram Naam Satya Hai. God is the only Truth.' The bier was hoisted.

The wind had dropped and a rank smell hung over the cremation ground. Jagu cleared a little space among the debris, dug a pit and filled it with dry wood, stick by stick. The dead body was placed on the pyre.

The moon suddenly broke from behind a bank of clouds as Jagu removed the veil from the woman's face. The gold nose-stud glittered in the moonlight.

A shiver ran down Jagu's spine.

The moon disappeared behind a cloud for a moment and sailed out again, the light and shadow playing hide-and-seek on the pale face of the corpse.

Jagu stretched his hand towards the jewel and stopped. The woman's face was like a wilting blue lily, her thick tresses resembled the clouds the moon was flirting with. Jagu felt a knot in his stomach.

The moon again slipped behind a cloud. Jagu waited. A lump rose in his throat. Why did he feel so sad? Had he not burnt enough young women? Why did he find the job so awful, so difficult this time? Many a woman had been prettier than this one.

He caught himself thinking about her. On her nose, she had a little trinket of gold and in her faintly swollen womb, an unborn child. Another four or five months and she would have become a mother. Why did she have to come to an end like this? It wasn't her fault her husband had deserted her within a fortnight of their marriage. It wasn't a crime to be young and vivacious, to thirst for love, to crave male caresses, to exult in the exalting passions of the flesh. Was it her fault that the repressed passion of her starved body had overcome her sense of right and wrong? What was right and what was wrong, anyway? Who could judge?

'Come on, Jagu!' the pallbearers fidgeted. 'Hurry up. The red turbans might swoop down on us any moment. Take the nose flower off the corpse and light the pyre. For heaven's sake, don't waste time.'

'I don't want that flower of evil,' Jagu said, coming out of his reverie. 'Let it go with her.'

'The golden nose-stud? Are you sure? All right, then torch the bitch. God knows how long she'll take.'

'Douse her with kerosene. It'll help.'

'Are you sure you don't want that piece of gold?' The pallbearers quizzed Jagu. 'How come?'

He did not say a thing.

The tongues of fire leaped up. The wood crackled. The body turned and twisted a little. The skin crinkled and turned black. Jagu's eyes remained riveted on the pyre. After about an hour, he took his stick and probed the lump. Soon it would be time to smash the skull. A sigh escaped him.

An owl began to hoot in the far corner of the cremation ground and vultures flapped their wings; a male jackal set up an eerie howl. The putrid stench of burning flesh hung thick in the air.

The cremation proved a smooth business. The rain held off. The pallbearers chatted gaily among themselves.

'Good for him, he didn't touch the tainted jewel of the whore,' remarked someone. 'That gold would have done Jagu no good.'

There was a chorus of agreement. Jagu winced.

'Whoever goes whoring around and killing the fruit of her womb,' said someone else, 'deserves a miserable end like this. There is *dharma*, after all, you know. You simply can't escape it.'

'Aw, shut the hell up,' Jagu Tiadi suddenly barked, a raw edge to his voice. 'Do me a favour and shut the hell up.'

KALINDI CHARAN PANIGRAHI

Victory Celebration

'Here you are, Manik,' Mukund said, as he barged into the house. 'Now boil these and stir up a good brew.'

'With how much water?' Manik asked, taking the bundle of dry roots from her brother.

'Not much, I guess. Half a bowl should do. But remember to take it off the heat before the water turns purple. Give Father a cup of it every so often. Oh, that reminds me, keep this lump of sugar. If he complains of being thirsty, give him a little drink of sweetened water.'

'What did Nidhi Maikap say? Father will get well, won't he?' The words seemed to pass her lips only with the greatest of efforts.

Critic Baishnab Charan Samal has dated the story to 1928. But this provenance does not seem correct. The story refers to the surrender of Japan that took place only at the end of the Second World War. The story was most likely written in 1945.

Undernourished and thin as a stick, at fifteen, she looked like a child of eight or nine.

'Of course, he will. Do you think I'd be running around if there was no hope? Old Nidhi Maikap—why, you should've seen how thrilled he was when I handed him his full fee of eight annas. "Don't worry, son," the country doctor said with a chortle. "This is a very potent concoction I've prepared for your father. If he doesn't sit up like a hale and hearty bear first thing tomorrow morning, then my name isn't Nidhi Maikap." That old windbag! But listen, Manik. He said Father must have one meal a day of rice gruel from tomorrow on. We'll need paddy for that. But then we don't have a grain of rice in the house, do we?'

Manik stopped in her tracks. She didn't know where in this god-forsaken village she could borrow or buy a measure. Even if somebody had a little stowed away, they wouldn't part with it for anything in the world, no matter how hard she banged her head against his door.

'Never mind,' said Mukund wearily. 'We'll think about that tomorrow. Now go and make the concoction.'

Nothing had been cooked since the night before and the fire had died in the oven. Manik pulled out a handful of straw from the thatch, twisted it into a thin strand and went out to borrow an ember from a neighbour.

Mukund tiptoed into the small dark room where his old ailing father, Guna Parida, lay dying. Six months had passed since he had taken to his bed. Meanwhile, his wife and two young sons had passed away within eight days of each other, bloating up horribly before dying. God alone knew what disease it was, but it took a heavy toll in the countryside: thousands of people had meekly succumbed to it. Man is born to die, thought Mukund. Sooner or later. So what did it matter? But this bland philosophizing irked him. Maybe his family could have scraped through with the proper medicine. But where was the money for that? The little he had was barely enough to buy rice for the sick.

Guna raised his withered hand and signalled him to sit down. Mukund slumped to the ground beside his bed. "Don't worry, son." Guna spoke in a hoarse whisper. "Just wait and see; I'll pull through."

Hope welled up in Mukund's heart. Yes, why not, he thought. Didn't old Maikap say the new potion would work wonders? A sigh escaped him. He had been able to do precious little for his mother and brothers; they had dropped dead before he knew what was happening. But he wouldn't let his father go the same way.

Guna Parida's four acres of land had dwindled to a small holding and what was produced was scarcely enough for the family. Like others, Guna had had to sell off chunks of land to survive. The rains had been unkind two years in a row and, as though that was not enough, the wartime government had declared Orissa a surplus state. It had squeezed the peasantry dry in its procurement drive and had sold off the entire rice stock beyond the borders, triggering a famine.

'Uma!' Guna stammered, staring blankly at his son. His mind was wandering.

Mukund winced as if scorched by a flame. In the early days of the famine, Uma—Guna Parida's eldest daughter, abandoned by her husband—had deserted her children and run off with another man, sullying the name of the Parida clan. Tongues had wagged; some said she had made straight for the poorhouse, others said she had become a whore. The incident had left indelible lines of shame and mortification on poor old Guna's heart. Why didn't the bitch drop dead? Mukund thought bitterly. Couldn't she find a drop of poison to put an end to her shameful life? Starvation and disease took so many people, why not her? Mukund always walked away when her name was spoken. Were his old father well, he wouldn't have hesitated to tell him what he thought.

'Is the brew ready?' he called out to Manik, ignoring the old man.

'In a moment,' Manik replied. After a while, she came in with a chipped stone bowl.

Guna took a small sip with great difficulty and shook his head. Manik set the bowl down on the floor near his pillow and left.

Outside, dusk had fallen. Clouds had thickened in the sky since afternoon and now a pitiful drizzle had started. The month of Shravan was on its way out, but there hadn't been a single good shower.

Manik went into the kitchen and found herself a clean white rag, rolled it into a wick and rubbed it in the bottom of an earthen bowl that had last seen oil ages ago. Oil had been the first thing to vanish from the wartime market.

'Anything to eat, little sister?' Mukund affected an exaggerated casualness.

'What!' A brief smile sprang to Manik's face, which resembled a withered bud. 'Oh yes, there's a little rice porridge from yesterday.'

'Good. You eat it up. It's your turn to keep watch over Father tonight.'

'But Brother, you haven't had anything since the day before yesterday!'

'Don't you remember the porridge you made the day before yesterday? Well, who ate most of it, if not me?'

Manik recalled having cooked a little porridge two days ago. It was a strange, outlandish dish, cooked out of three-day-old rice-water and yam leaves. 'But I'm sure you didn't touch any of it,' she said.

'Says who?' growled Mukund, rolling his large eyes, bloodshot from lack of sleep. 'Manik, are you my guardian, eh? Do I have to eat, sleep and do everything with you watching, or what? If I told you I've eaten, then I've eaten and that's all there is to it.' He was the hope of the family, he had overheard his parents saying, he was the bread winner. Pushing nineteen, Mukund was a strapping lad and ever since his father took to his bed, he had looked after the land—ploughing, digging and watering desperately. In happier circumstances, he would have been married by now. A rueful smile creased his face. His mother had looked forward to his wedding so much. But she was dead and gone and now Father too was sinking. Why should I let this slip of a girl boss me? 'Watch what you say, you little goose, when I ask you to do something. Who suffers from thirteen kinds of ailments in twelve months, little sister?' He tried to sound as gruff as a family patriarch. 'You're so thin that only a whiff of breeze would blow you away. And you talk about what I eat, hah! We men, we take a nibble whenever we can, of whatever we can lay our hands on, from flattened rice to rice puffs. But look at you. You said you had a bite this morning, didn't you? Now let's go out to the street and ask an outsider to take a look at the two of us and guess which one's starving. You know something, poor Ghania has yet to recover from last year's bruises, I pinned him down to the ground so hard. Now that's something I really enjoy—the bagudi competition during the Rajo Festival.' He gave a croak of a laugh. 'Sister, you'd better stop yapping.' Yesterday's rice porridge, he thought with a sigh. It must have fermented nicely by now. But I mustn't wolf it down. I must wait. Maybe Manik will save a little of it for tomorrow and cook it with a handful of broken rice and both of us can have a helping.

The sick man groaned hoarsely. Mukund and Manik hurried inside and propped him up against the wall. Guna had soiled himself. Manik fetched a rag and water and cleaned him up. Then she lit a wick in an earthen lamp and brought a bowl of sugar water for him. Guna refused to take more than a gulp.

They came out of the room. Mukund lifted a pitcher of water and poured it down his throat. 'I had some rice puffs, you know,' he said with a snort, forcing out a belch. 'They can make you damn thirsty, rice puffs can. I say there's nothing as good as water. Hunger or thirst, a bellyful of water takes care of everything. Sister, go have the rice porridge before it becomes inedible."

Manik tucked into the stale porridge without another word. 'Brother,' she said. 'You know something. The Jenas eat hot rice meals twice a day even now.'

Mukund let out another loud belch. 'Oh, don't envy others, my girl. What does it matter to us if they eat hot rice twice a day? Are you going to beg from them or what? Listen, I'm Guna Parida's son. Begging is not in our blood. We ate hot rice as long as we could. It's only for a month or so ...' He paused a while. 'Just wait until Father recovers. You can blame me if we don't have nice hot rice meals every second day. But if you think you can't wait any longer, then the doors of the poorhouse are wide open for you. One sister has already tarred our faces, you can go and keep her company. You'll come across quite a few familiar faces there, I'm sure.'

'Shut up, will you?' Manik cried. 'Why do you always fly into a temper when I tell you any little thing? I'm sick of your sermons.'

'Who asked you to bring up the Jenas? Remember, the stale cold watered rice of your own house is better any day than the sweet milk-porridge of somebody else's. What business is it of ours to know what others are eating?'

'Have you finished?'

'All right. Go to bed. I'll keep watch over Father the first half of the night. I'm not feeling sleepy. I'll wake you when I'm tired.'

Manik left.

Why do I take it out on the poor child? Mukund thought. Isn't it quite natural she should long for a bowl of hot rice? I can manage without food for three or four days at a stretch, that's no big deal for a man; scores of my friends are in the same condition if not worse. That reminds me, a little gruel has to be cooked tomorrow morning for Father. Where does one get a measure of old rice? Do I have to run to Banchha Sahu of Nuapara once again?

Banchha Sahu had given him an advance of five rupees against future wages, but Mukund had not been able to put in even a day's work because of the deaths in the family. How could he show his face at Sahu's and ask him for another advance? He briefly toyed with the idea of approaching the Jenas. But why waste his breath? There'd be nothing but a firm no from those quarters. When his mother was dying, he had gone and begged them for a lump of sugar, but old Jena was as cold as a stone. I'll be damned if I knock on his door a second time, thought Mukund. He recalled someone

Victory Celebration

mentioning Sadhu Panda of Manijangha and resolved to try his luck there.

'Manik, are you asleep? Get me the money bag from the hole in the wall, will you?'

Manik fetched him a small bundle wrapped in rags. He opened it and took out the money: two crumpled one-rupee notes and a handful of coins. That was all that was left of the advance.

'All right.' He handed Manik the notes. 'Put this back in the hole and block it up securely with a coconut shell. If rats or white ants get at it, we'll be done for. I'll take these nine annas and go to Manijangha tomorrow morning. Oh lord, a good four miles up and a good four down. And a big river of mud to wade through twice besides. Of course, I'll run as fast as the wind. Father must have a little rice gruel in his stomach tomorrow.'

'God knows how long it will take you.' Manik sighed. 'Last time you went to buy paddy, you took the whole day and bought no more than a rupee's worth.'

'That was different. You're talking about rations, sister. You know something, there were people who stood in line for three days and still returned home empty-handed. You should have seen the mile-long line to believe it. Distribution was slow and the queue crawled a foot an hour. You received your quota only when your turn came. No one would let you jump the queue. Don't ask me how I managed. Anyway, all that is over now. The government has refused to distribute further rations. It's different with Sadhu Panda. No hassles there. Pay cash, collect the rice and hit the road back home. By the way, tomorrow morning, you're not going to the swamps to collect marua rice. I want you to sit with Father.'

Of late, Manik had taken to visiting the swamps, carrying a wicker basket in her hand, to collect marua rice from the weeds. Not only she, but droves of women and children, hungry, emaciated and aggressive, made a beeline for the place, some getting up at ungodly hours to have a head start. Pausa had come and gone and the measly harvest—the third in a row—had not even been enough to satisfy the demands of the landlords. People had relied heavily on the bounties of the seasons: raw mangoes and yams in summer; fish, crabs and snails in the rainy months; different sorts of greens and leaves in and out of season; and now, before the onset of winter, marua rice. The swamps, mist hanging over them, presented a unique sight: waves of human beings billowing around the place, revealing a hand here, a bare back there, heads bobbing, wicker baskets swimming in the void.

Manik spread the end of her sari and lay down, curling up like a puppy. But sleep wouldn't come to Mukund. He was lost in his thoughts: my little sister is such a pathetic bag of bones and yet she drags herself every morning to the swamps. And I can do nothing about it. I've failed to go for work just for a few weeks and want has closed in on us from all sides. Will I be able to save Father? Will I be able to save Manik?

When Manik awoke before cockcrow next morning, she found her brother gone. She could feel a fever coming on, her body ached and her head felt as heavy as a stone. This was nothing new; she had had a fever off and on ever since last summer. She had never breathed a word of it to Mukund.

She heard her father stirring in his bed. She got up and went to him, washed his face with water and wiped it dry with her sari. 'Shall I get you a bowl of sugar water?' she asked.

Victory Celebration

Guna's eyes had sunk into their sockets. He raised his hand with the greatest of efforts and put it on his daughter's head. His lips trembled, but no word came out.

'Brother has gone to buy rice for gruel,' Manik said. 'He'll be back any moment now.'

It was high noon when Mukund bought two measures of rice and started his trudge back home. The road stretched ahead of him. He crossed the river at its narrowest; the mud still came up to his waist. When he reached the outskirts of his village, he lowered himself into a ditch to wash himself.

'That can wait,' said someone. 'But not your father. Run along home.'

Mukund swivelled around. It was Ghania. Was the fellow being spiteful? he wondered. 'Joking, boy?' he asked.

'Go find out for yourself,' Ghania said, pushing and prodding a herd of rickety cattle towards the grey grassless pastures.

'Brother, hey, do you still hold it against me, last summer's game of bagudi?' Mukund said. 'All right, I'm ready to accept the fault was mine. There, now forget the old grudge.'

'Run along, boy,' Ghania said, turning and twisting the tail of an old cow. 'You're wasting your breath.'

Mukund's hands and legs went dead. The sky seemed to collapse on his head; the ground sank under his feet. Fighting off the daze, he broke into a run. The breeze carried Manik's heart-rending sobs. He reached home, threw the bag down and slumped to the ground.

The paddy came in handy for his father's shraddha ceremony. He engaged a priest and went through all the rites—although in these hard times, nobody would have faulted him for negligence. He blew a full rupee and couldn't have cared less. His father had died and along with him Mukund's hopes and dreams. The wandering mendicant's songs over his doleful khanjani jarred on him. Life is an illusion, is it? he mused. Each passing day brought him more unhappiness.

Then one day, he overheard the village schoolmaster discussing the war: 'Oh, quit worrying. The end of the war is in sight. Japan is buckling. Prices will soon come down. Rice will once again be widely available.' When? Mukund wondered. Will I live to see it? Manik's fast sinking; how long can a young girl survive on a handful of rice flakes a day? How will she get back her strength without freshly cooked rice?

He had only one rupee left and he decided to spend it all on rice. He would leave the entire amount with Manik and go to work at the Sahu's. That seemed the most sensible course. But where will I manage to buy rice? Who's going to sell any? I'll have to go through many a village and knock on many a door. Never mind. I can't let my little sister end up in the poorhouse. If the teacher is to be believed, the war will be over soon. Then prices will fall and the market will overflow with rice. It's just a matter of scraping through until then. As if in determination, he tightened his threadbare towel around his waist.

Next morning, he set out early. While passing by the village cremation ground, his feet slowed down and he stopped. Heaps of bones littered the ground. Skulls rolled around like pumpkins; teeth bared in hideous grins. The wind whistled through the empty ribcages of the skeletons. Somewhere in these heaps, he thought, are the bones of my family. The bones of my mother and brothers. And now my father's. Soon I'll end up here. And maybe little Manik too. But the sweet old world will not stop turning, will it?

Victory Celebration

'Patra of Kusupur has hoarded mounds of paddy underground,' said someone.

Mukund looked up and found he had caught up with a small group of men and women hurrying along the dirt tracks.

'Then let's try his place first,' said another.

'If all of us head there, he'll shoo everyone away,' ventured a third.

Kusupur would have been nearer home, but Mukund was disheartened. He turned his eyes in the direction of Manijangha and his spirits dimmed. Four long miles there and four longer miles back, to speak nothing of the river of mud! He took a deep breath and plunged blindly ahead, picking out a path that wound towards Manijangha.

Late in the afternoon, exhausted, he re-crossed the river with a sack of paddy. His stomach rumbled and turned, his knees wobbled, he wanted to throw up and every four paces he stopped to catch his breath. The sun broke through the ragged clouds and blazed down. He thought his skull would split open. The last stretch of fields before the village cremation ground seemed vast and unending, the giant banyan tree on the edge of the village, a speck in the distance. He looked around and spotted a ditch. He ran there and gulped down a few mouthfuls of water. It was muddy and had an awful stink. Things will look up tomorrow, he thought, wiping his mouth. After that we will have one meal of steaming hot rice a day.

Then suddenly, before he knew what was happening, he retched. The sack rolled off his shoulder and he fell to the ground. Mustering the last dregs of his strength, he picked himself up, lifted the sack to his head and took a step. Just the fields to cross, he told himself. Just scramble up the canal bank and you're almost home. He took another step. His legs folded and a violent trembling seized him. The sack fell off his head. He wanted to throw up again and again, as nausea came over him in relentless waves. There was no one in sight. A thin white wisp of a cloud passed overhead, dropping a few futile drops of rain. A breeze sprang up. He opened his eyes and stared at his village. His strength was ebbing fast. Oh, no more walking for me, he sighed, no more worrying. His eyes smarted. He closed them, laying his head against the sack.

The fieldhands brought the news of his death to the village. Manik's fever dropped and she ran to the fields. Tears had dried in her eyes. Her brother had left her a bag of rice.

That evening the village chowkidar strode into the village, breathless with excitement. 'Japan has surrendered!' he announced. 'We've won the war. The government wants us to celebrate the victory with appropriate pomp. Go deck your doors with mango twigs and leaves. Sweets will be distributed to school children at the police station tomorrow morning.'

Mukund celebrated the victory no less than the rest, perhaps even more. This was his first chance to be carried on human shoulders—and also his last!

RAJKISHORE RAY

Bauli

It all began in the gathering twilight of an innocuous day when the old duffadar, a petty police official, on his way back from the police station, came across the narrow village path sandwiched between screw-pine bushes and climbed the steps to Bhajani Pradhan's veranda. He stooped a little, as if carrying on his ageing shoulders the enormous burden of a dozen or more lucrative schemes and plans—to encourage new lawsuits and find quick out-of-court settlements. The brass buttons of his uniform, scrubbed with ashes, gleamed. The bulging bundles of papers under his arm, held together between cardboard covers that had gone soft and from which a string limply hung, were dark from the inky stains of a million thumbprints.

Bhajani's wife, Sarasi, was sweeping the mud platform around the sacred basil plant in the courtyard when she saw him arrive. Quickly pulling the veil over her head, she fetched a reed mat and

---

'Bauli' was first published in 1945 in *Sahakar*, Vol. 25, No. 4.

spread it on the veranda. She was his goddaughter and his visits were a routine. Invariably, he would ask after her welfare and once the polite enquiries were over, gush about the aubergines in her vegetable patch, the thickness of Ujala's milk, the richness of Patani's cream—all of which he secretly hankered for.

Bhajani had hired himself out as a farmhand and raised a few head of cattle. But it was Sarasi who really looked after the animals. She was poor, but her heart was full of tenderness and devotion, for her husband and the cattle—Ujala, Patani, Manguli, all cows; Jagannath and Balabhadra, a pair of bullocks; and Bauli, a pretty little calf. They were the objects of her love. She was grateful to Goddess Lakshmi, whom she worshipped by painting a symbolic pattern of tiny footsteps in the eastern corner of her house, not only for a bountiful harvest, but for the health of her cattle too. At the crack of dawn, just when the sun's chariot rose in the sky, lighting the pale-blue horizon, she would tug at the udders of her cows and direct the jets into the pot balanced between her knees. The thrill of it was so pure, so satisfying, that it helped her bury deep within the recesses of her heart the pangs of childlessness—that most acute pain of womanhood. Indeed, neither her workaholic husband, nor the loving animals had any inkling of these feelings. As the vessel gradually filled to the brim with Ujala's milk—pure, snow-white and frothy—little Bauli's wet muzzle would nudge Sarasi's back, hands and arms. She found the touch so delicious that she often imagined how much more thrilling would have been the touch of a child of her own. In the village community hall, she had often heard the stories of the dalliances of Lord Krishna, of His life and pranks at Gopapur. She had been to the village shows put on by the untouchables and had watched the tears and suffering of

Jashoda overwhelmed with love for the young Krishna. She had been fascinated by the mischievous capers of the Lord behind the cattle in the streets of Gopa, the way He broke the milk pots with a slingshot and then the sudden fear of His mother, which made Him stand glued to the wall. Sarasi had absorbed every last detail. Where was her tiny toddler, scampering about on unsteady legs, smiles dimpling his chubby cheeks, playfully breaking the milk pot? It was a dream that never left her and the more the frisky Bauli carried on with her antics, the more she felt the lack of a child in her life.

'Daughter, where's Bhajani?' The duffadar was all smiles. 'Away in the fields, eh?'

'Yes,' said Sarasi, half-hidden behind the door. 'Must be on his way back now.' Knowing how much the old man loved flattened rice with curd made from Ujala's milk and fresh jaggery, she bustled about to get this ready for him.

'Sara,' the old man said, while doing justice to the spread, 'there'll be a live-stock fair in Cuttack. Why don't you ask Bhajani to take Ujala and Bauli? I'm sure the cow and the calf would steal the show. You've kept them so well-groomed, so scrubbed and polished that even flies would slip off their coats. They're a feast for the eyes. A prize-winning cow will fetch the owner a cash award of fifty rupees.'

'Fifty? How much is that?'

'Two score and ten.'

'So much!'

'Yes. Down at the police station, the chief told me to spread the word. Rural people should take part in large numbers. Arrangements have been made for food and shelter for the animals and their owners in the fair grounds. Remember to tell Bhajani. If I run into him on the way home, I'll try to convince him.'

'But it would be a waste of two precious days,' she remarked. 'And he would need money to spend for expenses on the way there. If he wins the prize, he'll get it only at the end, isn't that right?'

Panchu, with his dog Kalia in tow, had stopped to listen to them. Although Kalia was just a country dog with no pedigree to boast of, he was so fearless that at a nod from his master he'd attack a cow or a bull ten times his size. His devotion to Panchu and their love for each other had earned them the respect of the villagers.

'Panchu,' the duffadar said. 'Why don't you take Kalia to Cuttack? A brave dog like him stands a good chance of winning a prize.'

'He's a country dog,' Panchu said. 'Will anyone even look at him?' He ran his fingers over Kalia's head. The dog thumped his bushy tail on the ground and clawed up a little mud as though to suggest that he was game, that it was well worth taking a chance.

Kantha the priest had stopped by too. He was as famous for his evening services in the village Shiva temple as for slitting the throats of rams that defied the expertise of seasoned butchers. (For a fee of two rupees, he could decapitate the most obstinate goat or sheep; his patrons, mostly school and college students, were many. As a result, Kantha didn't lack for money.) This was a skill he had apparently picked up in Puri, where as a young boy he had gone to the local training centre for wrestling lessons. The vertical line of vermilion from the base of his hairline down to the tip of his nose was a nostalgic commemoration of his arduous training. The towel around his broad shoulders, rising and falling rhythmically with each step, had become a part of his self; it responded as much to his talk as to his walk and every time Kantha raised his voice, the ends of the towel twirled and danced.

'Priest,' the duffadar said. 'Make your ewe dance?'

'Want to see a performance? All right, all right.' Kantha slapped his arms and called to his dear ewe. Although it was a familiar sight, it always had an air of freshness about it because of the Puri slang, which was a part of Kantha's flow of words.

Kantha had brought up his ewe with great care and tenderness. It was a large animal, glossy black, the hair on its neck as deep and dense as a lion's mane; the horns curling around the sides of its head gave it the look of a warrior with lavish sideburns. Kantha spent more money on this animal than any man of comfortable means in the village did on himself. Madhav Mian, the local butcher, had once offered up to forty rupees for it, but Kantha had rejected the very idea.

Two days later, at the crack of dawn, a unique procession was seen on the riverbank: Kantha in front with his ewe at his side, followed by Panchu tugging at the rope around Kalia's neck, with Bhajani, Ujala and Bauli bringing up the rear.

In the huge animal and agricultural fairground in Cuttack, there was a noticeable contrast between the rugged, mud-splattered, hard-working, rumpled, swarthy villagers and the superficial polish of city slickers.

Lost amid all the faces, Panchu, Kantha and Bhajani wondered what it was all about. Their animals were hungry, tired and jittery. The ewe, startled by the sound of a motor horn, had twice snapped its rope; Ujala, a trudge of eighteen miles behind her, was unable to stand and had tears streaming down her cheeks; Bauli lay on her back, limp and exhausted, her legs stiff as sticks, although for a large part of the distance, Bhajani had carried the four-month-old calf on his shoulders. He had brought her up on a diet of green-gram powder, but in the town, nothing but hay was available. He had already appealed to one of the organizers only to be directed to another, who in turn had directed him to a third and so on. Bhajani had neither the energy nor the zeal to follow the trail.

Suddenly lusty shouts went up: 'The minister! The minister's car!'

Kalia was in a frenzy, since he had always reacted to sudden noise of any kind; he spied a brood of plump hens and began to bark his head off.

When the speeches began, the stomachs of Panchu, Kantha and Bhajani rumbled with hunger.

'Learn from Holland and Denmark.' The minister's voice resounded over the public address system. 'Look after your cows as they do in those countries. Feed them well and they will multiply. And yield more milk, too. Several writings on cattle-rearing are available nowadays. Read and profit from them. We have with us today a Denmark-trained cow-expert, who will enlighten you on how to build an ideal cowshed. We have another expert to provide a full explanation of the methods of poultry-farming . . .'

Words, words and more words. The three friends had listened to it all. They couldn't see the minister from where they were and wondered what a minister looked like.

'An important announcement!' The microphones rumbled on. 'The Hon'ble Minister congratulates the department of agriculture for making this fair a grand success and as a token of his appreciation, he shall now present a cash reward of one hundred rupees to the employees of the department.'

Bauli

Once the speeches were finally over, the prize-winners were declared: Paata, owned by the mahant of Cuttack, was the best cow; deputy magistrate Bhattacharya's bitch, Lily, the best dog; My Darling, the best ewe of Abu Hassan—a prominent businessman in the city—the best sheep; somebody else's goat the best goat.

The three hopefuls, who had come a distance of thirty-six miles, listened to the announcements in silence. Panchu and Bhajani stared at each other and Kantha's eyes were fastened on someone who was none other than the meat king of Cuttack, Sharif Khan. Khan's sharp business antenna was seeking out signals and his roving eyes were sizing up the animals for likely transactions. Animals could be had for a song after the fair.

Panchu, Kantha and Bhajani were in the throes of despair. They had no money and the prospect of trudging back another thirty-six miles made their heads reel. The twelve and a half annas Sarasi had given Bhajani had been spent on fodder for Ujala and Bauli and on a measure of flattened rice for himself and his companions. Kantha had some money of his own, but all of that had been spent on opium, which he couldn't do without.

The country dog, Kalia, was not a saleable commodity. Panchu was safe. Ujala and Bauli, the mother and the daughter, were an inseparable part of Bhajani's life. That left only Kantha's ewe—Sharif Khan's eyes had never strayed from this magnificent animal—and Kantha sold his beloved animal for five rupees. The raging fire of hunger in his and his two friends' stomachs had to be put out.

The return journey was made in total silence; no one had a word to say. Bhajani's shoulders, red and raw, hurt from carrying Bauli all the way from the fairground. The poor little calf, its belly distended, was in terrible shape. She groaned constantly and brought up blood with every cough. Behind them, Ujala limped, dragging her hind legs; the tears that had been flowing since she had left the village had never dried up. At every little opportunity, Kalia put his muzzle beside her ears and sniffed.

A few hours later, Bhajani put Bauli down on the ground. 'It's all over for the little one,' he said.

Panchu and Kantha stopped.

The poor calf was dead. The trickle of blood with which her life had ebbed out was all there was to see.

Bhajani raised his head and looked at the sky. It was teeming with stars. 'Kantha,' he cried out, his voice catching. 'Priest, how will I face Sara? What will I tell her? Will she survive the shock? Can I stop her from hitting her head against the wall? God didn't give her a child, but He had given her Bauli. The little calf was her daughter.'

Kantha wiped the long vermilion line off his forehead; he would never wear it again. 'Bhajani, brother, roll Bauli down the riverbank and forget her. The fair's over. She didn't matter. Neither did we.'

Only Kalia hung back where Bauli's carcass was abandoned. With his head bowed, he stood rooted to the spot.

RAJKISHORE PATTANAIK

A House to Let

Of all the houses that Batakrushna passed on his way to college, some very beautiful and elegant, the one he found arresting was low and thatch-roofed, damp and in an advanced state of decay. Situated on a vacant lot full of shrubs and bushes—the nearest houses on either side were at least a couple of hundred feet away—it stood out.

On a day of heavy rain, with torrents of water, the colour of red mud gushing onto the road—a nearby pond was already overflowing—Batakrushna fell off his bicycle right in front of this house.

After he had picked himself up, soaked to the skin, he noticed a young woman watching him from the doorway. Her eyes were still; there was not a trace of laughter, let alone a hint of ridicule on that beautiful face.

'Bhadaghara', according to the author, was written in 1945, but was published in an eponymous anthology in 1958.

He was annoyed with himself for having chosen that particular spot to fall off his bike, but instead of hurrying away, he wanted to stop and straighten the handlebars and take shelter from the downpour on the veranda of the house. If only she would invite him.

But the young woman's gaze remained as distant and immobile as before.

As he crossed the flooded patch, Batakrushna craned his neck one time too many to take in more of the woman—the sole witness to his shame, embarrassment and pain.

Back home, as he changed into dry clothes and warmed his damp bed, he caught himself fantasizing about her. In his fond imagination, she'd already become an object of desire.

From then on, he shunned all other routes to and from college and stuck to the same one, hoping to catch occasional glimpses of her.

But for a long time, he didn't see her again. He made it a point to ring the bell on his bicycle, often without any cause, but no one ever appeared in the doorway. The drain that ran in front of the house always reminded him of the heavy downpour, the flooded road and his ignominious fall. And his hope of seeing the girl again remained just that—a distant hope.

A month passed. One evening, he saw two women coming out of the house, one of them the girl he was longing to see. As their eyes met, he was pleased to see a flicker of recognition in her eyes. Her eyes had lit up as if spotting a familiar face in a crowd.

But the girl seemed tired, worn-out, no longer as fresh and lively as she had been on that first day. Judging by the clothes she and her companion wore, they were not very well-off. What had happened to her? Batakrushna's mind was racing. Could worries and anxiety have reduced her to this? No, some prolonged illness more likely. What else could explain why he hadn't seen her all this time?

His anger rose against the house, growing by the day. The low thatch-roofed house with its damp walls had brought sickness to his beloved, the object of his dreams.

From then on, he sometimes saw her at the door. Her face remained as impassive and immobile as ever and her eyes as remote and unseeing. But he'd find himself blushing heavily and his heart beating wildly at her sight. He'd apply more pressure to the pedals to push past the house as fast as he could.

In the course of time, on his way back and forth, he slowed down so he could study the house a little further, drinking in more of its air and ambience. He began to take note of the vegetable vendors, paanwallahs, house repairers, travelling salesmen and others who called there; their faces became familiar in his mind like imprints branded on wet clay pots.

He began to like many aspects of the house, but the girl remained as remote as in the past.

As if ordained by fate, when he was passing by a few days later, he saw a horse-drawn carriage laden with luggage leaving the house. His heart gave a lurch; somebody seemed to whisper into his ears: she's leaving forever. He could see the rounded elbow of a woman sticking out the carriage window. He followed it for some distance but stopped when it seemed to him an unseemly and indecent act. He knew he'd lost for all time to come the girl he'd got used to dreaming about.

In the days that followed, as he pushed past the house, he took to checking up on it. It remained locked. Still, he lived in a fog of hope. Maybe the object of his romantic feelings would come back someday soon.

Only she never did. And the house for rent remained firmly shut and locked.

Batakrushna continued to pass by the house day after day after day. He let his fantasies grow more beguiling, changing shape and size; he was in their thrall.

Then one day, he found strangers had moved into that familiar place. He felt he was being dragged away from the girl of his dreams. He began to look upon the house for hire with contempt and loathing—the way a jilted lover would.

But before long, he discovered the woman that had moved in was none other than Surekha, someone he knew. Five years ago, she had married and moved away with her husband.

One day he met her. Surekha fished in her basket of memories and poured out the stories of her joys and sorrows. And her complaints too: her husband was poor, his salary meagre.

Perhaps she had already grown cold and indifferent towards her husband and seemed to like Batakrushna more. Sitting and chatting with her, he imagined her to be the woman he was still in love with and dreamt of. Thus, for wholly different reasons, they came closer, each feeding the other with stories of unrequited love.

Then Surekha's son fell ill. The illness worsened by the day. Because they couldn't afford to buy all the medicine, he died within three days. Surekha blamed his death on the house: the rented house had plucked her boy from her lap. Her loyalties swung back from Batakrushna to her husband again. In the moments of her acute sorrow, Batakrushna had merely mouthed a few platitudes, a few superficial words of consolation, no more

A House to Let

than lip-service, whereas her husband had hugged her and cried his heart out too.

Batakrushna continued to visit Surekha because by now she had replaced his object of love in his mind. But more than her, it was the house that seemed to have cast a spell on him. His attraction towards it was inexplicable.

All of a sudden, Surekha and her husband moved, leaving with all their belongings. Once again, the door remained shut and a lock dangled from it.

This was the second jolt Batakrushna had been dealt with.

From then on, every time he passed by it, he felt that the derelict house, with its crumbling walls and disintegrating floor, was mocking him. His heart no longer raced as he rode past. His eyes remained distracted even as he tried to focus. Sometimes he wished he could buy and demolish the house, or have it refurbished. His bittersweet dreams and fantasies began growing wings again. He stopped imagining that the house was hexed, that it only brought grief to anyone who rented it.

After a long, long time, Batakrushna's friend Damodar rented the house and moved in. He was very poor and dying of tuberculosis and planning to live there during the course of his treatment.

Now Batakrushna began to fear the house. Not just the four walls, but everything about it, the very air around it. He could no longer step inside it as joyfully as he'd have liked to, tormented as he was by the memories of his first love and then of Surekha. Death seemed to inhabit the place. He couldn't help but notice his friend's inexorable descent to his end. Whenever his sick friend looked up at him, Batakrushna, himself so hale and hearty, was full of foreboding. He was wracked by fear and worry that like Surekha's young boy, his poor friend would die in this house. The house had got rid of his first love too. Now it was getting ready to devour his friend.

After Damodar breathed his last in that ramshackle house, Batakrushna began to avoid that route. But whenever he had unavoidable reasons to ride by, he couldn't help but notice the house remained under lock and key. There were no new takers for it. The news of the death of the last tenant from tuberculosis had spread and no one was willing to rent it any longer.

Batakrushna moved away too. But occasionally, when he passed by the house for rent, he was filled with revulsion and loathing. It no longer revived the memories of his dreams and fantasies. He still remembered the faces of all those who had once lived there, but none of his recollections brought him any joy.

SURENDRA MOHANTY

Australia

M‍Y POCKET IS empty but for a counterfeit quarter-rupee coin lying deep in its remotest folds.

That's all I possess in this whole wide world of two billion people—just this one useless counterfeit coin.

But still the tea seller is so kind and polite. He's already let me drink tea on credit—not just one, but three cups of tea, since the morning. The cigarette vendor is no less kind and generous. He knows I'm down and out and has never demanded the money I owe him.

The street . . . The main street of the town, heaving with passersby, everyone with dreams and hopes. An unceasing flow of people from morning until night.

I am part of the flow—of the flotsam, the debris. And I have my pocketful of dreams . . . Such as sailing off to faraway Australia. That's my dream. There are reports of a new gold mine just discovered down under.

'Australia' was first published in 1945 in *Sahakar*, Vol. 25, No. 6.

My dreams quickly grow wings.

I float a large joint stock company in Australia, the seed capital runs into several million rupees. I acquire a monopoly on the prospecting and mining rights ... Australia ... that far-off land ... ropes of thick black smoke curling out of the tall chimneys of the smelting plants of the Kalgoorlie gold mine in the middle of a vast expanse of arid desert where even nomadic sheep-herders lose their way, especially on stormy nights ...

Along the road, I watch the procession of the hungry, the naked and the deprived ... in their hundreds ... old, young, boys and children, men and women, with or without sight, all bent and broken by life ...

'Allah will shower His blessings on you ...'

'May God add millions of years to your life ...'

God's grace and Allah's blessings are a dime a dozen! One can buy lots of that for less than a paisa. They seem to be the cheapest commodity on sale.

The merchant retailing Allah's blessings is a derelict—leprosy-stricken, old, crippled—who's leaning against the lamppost, his cloth shoulder bag crowded with the one thing he sells: Allah's blessings. The fez on his head is so ancient that no one can say for sure what colour it once was. His face is intricately crisscrossed with crooked wrinkles, his eyes rheumy and streaming; he's clad in a ragged, discoloured overall of uncertain provenance.

'Allah will shower His blessings on you, son ...'

Not far from where he sells his wares is an old crone seated with her merchandise on a threadbare piece of jute sacking. 'May God add millions of years to your life ...'

Seems quite a few have already bought what she is peddling: a long life running to millions of years! In the rusted tin can she has set in front of her, there are already a few two-paisa coins. Quite a take—about three annas, if not more.

In my pocket, there's only a counterfeit quarter-rupee coin.

I'm spoilt for choice: God's grace or Allah's blessings?

Better than either will be a cup of tea. But I have to wait until the gloom of the evening, when I can hope to slip the coin into some unsuspecting tea seller's till.

I turn off the main street and enter a narrow lane into the underbelly of the town.

The mellow sunshine of a wonderful morning, the clear, expansive and generous autumn sky make me think of the auspicious glances of a shy new bride.

The shadows of the houses lie aslant on the red mud path of the quiet lane.

Perth. The bustling port of Perth. The ship from Bombay finally docks at Perth.

A long voyage across the Indian Ocean—on waters without borders or limits—as expansive as it is generous. Blue waves with foamy white crests; bobbing seagulls, with drops of water wetting their sun-baked wings... the port of Perth. The stench of sweat of deckhands and porters, the acrid smell of tobacco, the odour of unknown bodies, the smell of Australia... an indefinable smell of the unknown... ah, wonderful...

I reach Amir Khan Lane. The road sign is scribbled in tar on a piece of tin nailed to a peeling wall—the immortality bestowed by the twentieth century. In a subcontinent where millions of years can be added to one's life or Allah's eternal blessings can be had for a two-bit coin, a sign painted on a scrap of tin can definitely be the emblem of immortality.

'Dear darling Amir Khan, did ye know

Time carries away in a second all health, wealth and fame?

Ha, ha, ha! The port of Perth and Amir Khan Lane, the contrast, ha, ha, ha!

In the gurgling open drains on either side of the lane, the morning effluents gush forth, carrying the carcass of a kitten, scraps of letters and papers, twigs and pieces of straw. The blatant ridicule of the Indian Ocean recreated in the soapy, frothy wavelets of morning ablutions ejected from the town bathrooms. The contrast couldn't be more telling.

I catch sight of an ugly dark skeleton of a boy—must be a Harijan, God's people, so christened by Mahatma Gandhi, no less—rummaging in the filthy gutter for something. A Harijan boy. Oh God, what a travesty! How low can one get! Ha, ha, ha!

The boy, brought up short at my raucous laughter, eyes me with deep suspicion; his yellowing eyes, bloodless and dull, dim from fear.

Seems it'll take me a lot of exploration to complete my discovery of India. A long way to go. This is just the middle of the twentieth century. The industrial revolution has thrown up unheard-of business possibilities, an array of commercial ventures. Topping the list is of course the brisk sales of 'Allah's blessings' and 'God's grace.' What treasure was the Harijan boy rummaging for in the gutter? A safety-pin, a blunt discarded knife, what? Someday when God becomes a little more protective of his chosen people, the boy might land a quarter-rupee coin or maybe even a half-rupee, who knows!

There are as yet many undiscovered aspects that will make their way into a new manual—an enlarged and updated *Discovery of India*.

Australia

The counterfeit quarter-rupee coin slips through a hole in my pocket. No great loss, this loss of a fake coin in a big, bustling, heartless world. But the irony produces a strange sense of elation—a sharp thrill.

The strange, broken sound of the fake nickel coin hitting the earth—a rupture in the ghostly silence of the lane.

The Harijan boy jumps out of the gutter, swoops down on the coin like a hawk and runs for dear life.

What a look of triumph in his eyes.

His watchful eyes linger on me.

Those two eyes brim with contempt and suspicion. He doesn't trust me: I might snatch his prize from his hand. He throws the coin into his cavernous mouth.

And before I can say Jack Robinson, he's off like an arrow. As if he needs to put a wide berth between himself and a predator.

I walk to the end of Amir Khan Lane. Beyond it lies the scavengers' colony. Who do I see but that boy standing by the crumbling porch of a dilapidated hut strewn with the tiny white flowers of the nearby drumstick tree . . . what a lovely sight. With a lighted bidi clamped between his lips, he seems to be enjoying the smoke.

As soon as he catches sight of me advancing towards him, he scoots off into the jungle of rundown huts. And with him disappears my dreams of golden Australia . . . oh my Australia full of gold mines . . .

Two o'clock in the morning. The moon lies wan and anaemic in the sky. Sleep has completely vanished from my two eyes.

Australia . . . oh, land of gold . . . oh, Australia . . . land of my dreams . . .

If I ever get down to writing my autobiography and I single out one individual to devote a full chapter to, it'll have to be none other than Naseer, the cigarette vendor who's never hesitated to extend me a line of credit.

Lighting a cigarette, I walk back again to Amir Khan Lane. I don't know what pulls me to it, I simply can't resist.

Once again, I hit the scavengers' colony. The Harijan inhabitants are all blissfully asleep, without a bloody care, secure in God's dusty but capacious lap.

I notice the drumstick tree. It casts an eerie shadow in the moonlight.

Spread-eagled underneath the tree sleeps the boy I'd run into in the morning. On a gunny sack. A sliver of moonlight across his body.

What a beautiful night . . . so tender, peaceful, generous, soft.

It strikes me that today has been a great day—a day of great joy and happiness. Did this feeling of mine wash over the boy too and put him to such sound sleep?

Sleep has deserted my dry eyes, but . . .

Australia . . . land of gold . . . Australia . . . land of my golden dreams . . .

I'm far from falling asleep.

I inch closer and bend over the boy sleeping on his pitiful bed under the drumstick tree. In his unclenched fist I can see the counterfeit quarter-rupee coin shining in the moonlight. I can see a wan little smile on the boy's scarred, scared lips.

I step back. I retrace my steps.

The moon grows pale like the counterfeit quarter-rupee coin.

ACKNOWLEDGEMENTS

Our grateful thanks to:

Above all, Mini Krishnan, the godmother of Indian translations, who roped us in and who, without breathing down our necks, nudged us to respect the deadline; friends like Sudhansu Mohanty, Suman Dash, Asit Mohanty, Narendra Narayan Dash and Debatosh Acharya, who helped us with suggestions and materials; and the website odiabibhaba.in, the finest archival source of Odia books and journals in digital form, without which it would have been next to impossible to correctly ascertain the provenance of most of these early Odia stories.

We owe a debt of gratitude to Kartik Chauhan, our young, energetic, and deeply committed copy editor at HarperCollins. His meticulous attention to detail has been invaluable. We must also thank Rahul Soni, HarperCollins's commissioning editor, who initiated this series, rescuing from obscurity many important voices from the early decades of modern storytelling in Indian languages. May his tribe increase.

NOTES ON AUTHORS

Bankanidhi Patnaik (1889–1945) was a distinguished headmaster of his time. He published a collection of short stories, *Dhupachhaya*, besides a considerable body of children's books, translations and assorted non-fiction.

Bhagabati Charan Panigrahi (1907–1943), younger brother of Kalindi Charan Panigrahi, is remembered for his lone collection of stories, *Shikar*, which was published posthumously. A communist by political persuasion, he spearheaded popular revolts against the British imperial rule.

Biswanath Rath remains beyond the pale of literary history, which is surprising because he wrote a number of significant stories, which were published in *Nab Bharat* and in other journals like *Sahakar* and *Mukur* during the late 1930s and early 1940s.

Fakir Mohan Senapati (1843–1918), acknowledged as the father of modern Odia prose, wrote four novels, two collections of short stories, an autobiography and several essays, besides textbooks and a book of verse. His novel, *Chha Mana Atha Guntha*, is considered a foundational text of Indian literature. He also translated the Ramayana and the Mahabharata into Odia.

Godavarish Mishra (1886–1956) was born into a very poor family. He did all it took to have an education and took his BA and MA degrees from Ravenshaw College and Calcutta University at the top of his class. An acolyte of Utkalmani Pandit Gopabandhu Das, he taught at the Satyabadi National School, actively participated in the freedom movement and engaged in social activities. His *Collected Works* have been issued in five volumes. In the early 1950s, he served as a cabinet minister of Odisha.

Godavarish Mohapatra (1899–1965) wrote seventy books in a literary career that began at the early age of fourteen. Besides writing poetry, short stories, novels, humorous and satirical writings, belles-lettres, one-act plays, children's literature, as well as journalistic pieces, he edited and published *Nianakhunta*, a widely read satirical journal—from 1939 until his death in 1965. *Maguni's Bullock Cart* has been adapted into an award-winning film.

Gopinath Mohanty (1914–1991), younger brother of Kanhu Charan Mohanty, was the winner of the inaugural Sahitya Akademi Award in 1955 and the Jnanpith Award in 1974. His major novels include *Paraja, Danapani, Amrutara Santana, Laya Bilaya, Harijan* and *Dadi Budha*, all of which have also been translated into English. He was awarded the Padma Bhushan in 1991. His prodigious output in a literary career spanning almost half a century included not only twenty novels but also sixteen collections of short stories, besides an incomplete autobiography in three volumes and several translations, including Leo Tolstoy's *War and Peace* and Maxim Gorky's *My Universities*.

Harischandra Badal (1904–1995) was born in Balasore. Well-versed in several languages, including Sanskrit and Persian, he wrote prolifically during the 1930s and 1940s. A railway officer at a senior level, he spent a large part of his working life outside Odisha. The Odisha Sahitya Akademi published his *Collected Works* in 2022.

Kalindi Charan Panigrahi (1901–1991), novelist, short story writer, poet, critic and journalist, was educated in Ravenshaw College, Cuttack. Among his five novels is *Matira Manisha*, available in translation in English (*Salt of the Earth*, 2022) and fourteen other Indian languages. He published four collections of stories, which include *Sagarika*, *Rasiphala* and *Sesha Rashmi*. A long-time executive member of PEN, Sahitya Akademi and many other literary institutions, Panigrahi was honoured with the Padma Bhushan.

Kanhu Charan Mohanty (1906–1994) was a bestselling novelist of his time. Many of his novels, namely *Kaa* and *Janjha* and *Shashti*, have been made into popular films. He won several literary awards, among them the Sahitya Akademi Award.

Laxmikanta Mahapatra (1888–1953), better known as *Kanta Kabi* for his lyrical poetry, was educated in Cuttack and Calcutta and graduated from Ravenshaw College in 1913. From early youth, he suffered from leprosy, which put paid to his higher studies and shut him out from active participatation in the freedom movement, for which he had the greatest sympathy. His unfinished novel, *Kanamamu*, remains a firm favourite of young Odia readers. His contribution to children's literature is considerable. He founded *Dagar*, a major literary journal of the '50s and penned the state anthem of Odisha.

Nityananda Mahapatra (1912–2013), son of Laxmikanta Mahapatra, had no formal education, having dropped out of school early in life. He was the author of six novels and more than five collections of stories. He received the National Sahitya Akademi Award (1987) for his novel *Gharadiha*. Politically active until 1970, he served as a cabinet minister in Orissa in the late 1960s.

Rajkishore Pattanaik (1917–1997) was a lawyer by occupation and a writer by passion. His prodigious literary output included over five hundred short stories and several novels. Together with his sister Basant Kumari Pattanaik, who too was a writer, he ran a publishing venture for a few years.

Rajkishore Ray (1914–1998) was educated in the universities of Patna and Calcutta. He taught for over thirty years in various colleges before joining the directorate of higher education. He authored fourteen collections of short stories and a book of one-act plays. *Madhyannar Marupathe, Panka-chandan, Manar Mrunala, Bikacha Satadal, Bana Jyotsna* are some of his well-known collections of stories.

NOTES ON AUTHORS

Reba Ray (1875–1957) founded *Asha*, the first women's journal in Odia. Her story 'The Sanyasi', published in March 1899, six months after Fakir Mohan Senapati's 'Rebati', has the distinction of being the first modern Odia short story written by a woman. Her stories were collected in *Shakuntala* (1904). But soon she switched her loyalty to poetry and published several collections. A dedicated teacher and an activist, she founded the first high school for girls in Odisha. She also authored the first cookbook in Odia, *Randhana Pranali*, which came out in 1901.

Satchidananda Routray (1916–2004) is considered to have ushered in the post-modern period of Odia poetry. He received the Sahitya Akademi Award 1964 and the Jnanpith Award 1986. His short stories have been collected in five volumes. His 1934 picaresque novel, *Chitragriba*, is considered the first anti-novel in Odia literature. He was awarded the Padma Shri in 1962.

Suprabha Kar (1900–1982), daughter of Biswanath Kar, the eminent founder-editor of *Utkal Sahitya*, and an early female graduate, wrote prolifically in her early twenties. Her stories, poems and translations were all published in *Utkal Sahitya*. Inexplicably, she dropped off the literary map as soon as she married and moved to Calcutta.

Surendra Mohanty (1922–1990) was a short-story writer, novelist, critic, biographer and journalist. His four novels include *Andha Diganta* and *Nila Shaila*, for which he received the Sahitya Akademi Award in 1970. He published eleven collections of short stories, a two-volume history of Odia literature, critical works on Fakir Mohan Senapati, a two-volume biography of Madhusudan Das, the architect of modern Odisha, a travelogue and an autobiography. Engaged in active politics for over three decades, he was twice elected as a Member of Parliament to the Lok Sabha. He also edited the dailies *Kalinga* (1966–70) and *Sambad* (1988–90).

Upendra Kishore Das (1901–1972) was a writer, editor and painter whose enduring fame rests on the novel *Mala Janha* (*Dead Moon*), which was made into an award-winning film. A posthumous collection of his stories scattered in several literary journals of the 1920s and '30s is being readied for publication later this year. He translated Kalidasa's *Meghduta* and Jaydev's *Geet Govinda* and received the 1962 Sahitya Akademi Award for Translation.

NOTES ON THE TRANSLATORS

LEELAWATI MOHAPATRA's novel, *Hanging by a Tail*, was published in 2005. She has co-translated with K.K. Mohapatra and Paul St-Pierre extensively from Odia into English. Their works include: *The HarperCollins Book of Oriya Short Stories* (1998); *Ants, Ghosts and Whispering Trees: An Anthology of Oriya Short Stories* (2003); *The Greatest Odia Stories Ever Told* (2019); Fakir Mohan Senapati's *Six and a Third Acres* (2021) and Kalindi Charan Panigrahi's *Salt of the Earth* (2022).

PAUL ST-PIERRE is a former Professor of Translation Studies at Montreal University. He has co-edited several books on translation theory and practice and has spent over a quarter of a century collaborating with—apart from the Mohapatras—several Odia translators such as Ganeshwar Mishra, Basant Kumar Tripathy,

NOTES ON THE TRANSLATORS

Debendra Dash, Dipti Ranjan Patnaik and Himanshu Sekhar Mohapatra.

K.K. (KAMALAKANTA) MOHAPATRA has written three collections of short stories, a novel, a volume of essays and three books of memoir in Odia. He has translated into Odia works by Isaac Bashevish Singer, Gabriel García Márquez, Jean-Paul Sartre, Franz Kafka, William Shakespeare and others.

ABOUT THE SERIES EDITOR

Mini Krishnan

MINI KRISHNAN worked with Macmillan India Limited (1980–2000) and Oxford University Press (2000–18), editing textbooks for the Indian school market, and literary translations. She has co-authored textbooks for the Translation Education industry: *Word Worlds; Words, Texts & Meanings; Wordscapes*; and *Short Fiction from South India* (all published by Oxford University Press) and edited two volumes of translated fiction for the Aleph Book Company: *Tell Me a Long, Long Story* (sourced from fourteen languages) and *The Greatest Tamil Stories*. She is the series editor of *Living in Harmony*, a programme of peace education textbooks for schools (Oxford University Press).

She is currently Managing Editor of the Tamil Nadu Textbook and Educational Services Corporation, working with twenty English-language publishers to take Tamil to the world through translations of poetry, fiction and non-fiction, and on the editorial board of the Murty Classical Library of India, Harvard University Press.

She writes for *The Hindu* and *The Indian Express* and selects short stories in translation for the *Frontline* magazine.

HarperCollins *Publishers* India

At HarperCollins India, we believe in telling the best stories and finding the widest readership for our books in every format possible. We started publishing in 1992; a great deal has changed since then, but what has remained constant is the passion with which our authors write their books, the love with which readers receive them, and the sheer joy and excitement that we as publishers feel in being a part of the publishing process.

Over the years, we've had the pleasure of publishing some of the finest writing from the subcontinent and around the world, including several award-winning titles and some of the biggest bestsellers in India's publishing history. But nothing has meant more to us than the fact that millions of people have read the books we published, and that somewhere, a book of ours might have made a difference.

As we look to the future, we go back to that one word—a word which has been a driving force for us all these years.

Read.